EBURY PRESS

SIVAKAMI'S VOW: BOOK 1
PARANJYOTHI'S JOURNEY

Ramaswamy Krishnamurthy (1899–1954), better known by his pen name Kalki, was an editor, writer, journalist, poet, critic and activist for Indian independence. Kalki's expansive body of work includes editorials, short stories, film and music reviews, and historical and social novels. His stories have been made into films, such as *Thyaga Bhoomi* (Land of Sacrifice, 1939), the M.S. Subbulakshmi-starrer *Meera* (1945), *Kalvanin Kadhali* (The Thief's Lover, 1955), *Parthiban Kanavu* (Parthiban's Dream, 1960) and, most recently, the Mani Ratnam-directed *Ponniyin Selvan* (Ponni's Beloved, 2022). One of the most renowned names in Tamil literature, Kalki was awarded the Sahitya Akademi award for his novel *Alai Osai* (The Sound of the Waves).

Born and raised in Chennai, Nandini Vijayaraghavan is a director and head of research at the Singapore office of Korea Development Bank. Her translation of Kalki's *Parthiban's Dream* (2021) was shortlisted for a Valley of Words award in 2022. Nandini's columns on finance and economy have appeared in *BusinessLine*, *The Hindu*, *Economic and Political Weekly* and *Financial Express*. *Unfinished Business* (Penguin Random House India, 2023) is her first India-centric business book. Nandini co-authored a non-fiction book, *The Singapore Blue Chips* (2017), with Umesh Desai. Nandini blogs at www.litintrans.com.

SIVAKAMI'S VOW

BOOK I

PARANJYOTHI'S JOURNEY

KALKI

Translated from the Tamil by

NANDINI VIJAYARAGHAVAN

An imprint of Penguin Random House

EBURY PRESS

USA | Canada | UK | Ireland | Australia
New Zealand | India | South Africa | China

Ebury Press is part of the Penguin Random House group of companies
whose addresses can be found at global.penguinrandomhouse.com

Published by Penguin Random House India Pvt. Ltd
4th Floor, Capital Tower 1, MG Road,
Gurugram 122 002, Haryana, India

First published in Ebury Press by Penguin Random House India 2023

10 9 8 7 6 5 4 3 2 1

ISBN 9780143460022

Typeset in Adobe Caslon Pro by MAP Systems, Bengaluru, India
Printed at Replika Press Pvt. Ltd, India

www.penguin.co.in

Contents

Foreword

Of the three historical novels that Kalki R. Krishnamurthy wrote, *Sivakamiyin Sabadham* remains my favourite. I am aware that die-hard fans of *Ponniyin Selvan* (should I refer to it now as PS?) will raise their eyebrows, but then there it is. It probably is my favourite because it was the first Kalki novel that I read—I must have been seven or so, and had just then acquired fluency in reading Tamil. My grandmother, who had taught me the language, was happy with my choice. She was a sort of censor for the household when it came to reading matter in Tamil, and the magazine *Kalki* was one of the few periodicals that was permitted. Even in the 1970s, it was ultra-respectable; I know, for instance, that it refused cigarette advertisements, tempting though they might have been for a magazine that did not have deep pockets.

And so, I read *Sivakamiyin Sabadham*, eagerly awaiting the installments as they appeared in the weekly issues of the magazine. By then, Kalki the author was long dead. He was, however, a familiar face as his picture appeared on the editorial page, issue after issue. Twenty years after his passing, he was still the human face of the magazine, to which he had lent his pen name. And the re-serialization of his works remained the stock-in-trade of the publication. He seemed evergreen. That he was able to captivate a boy of seven, thirty years after he wrote the novel, spoke much about his awesome capabilities. Later, I read many of his other works—his historical and social novels, his short stories and, years later, when I took to music research, his reviews of concerts, plays and films, and above all, his writings championing Tamil as a musical language. I became a Kalki fan and remain one.

Why did *Sivakamiyin Sabadham* appeal to me more than any other of his works? I am unable to put a finger on it. The broad lines of the plot were clearly inspired by the Ramayana and *The Iliad*—it was the genius of Kalki that he was able to bring it all together in an entirely different context and setting. Then there is the characterization—always a strong point with Kalki. In school history textbooks, the Pallavas were a line or two, but those of us who had read our Kalki knew that there was much more to them. For many of us, *Sivakamiyin Sabadham* was an introduction to Kanchi, Mamallapuram, Badami and, above all, to Thirunavukkarasar, the great savant and hymnodist, one of the sixty-three saints of the Shaivite canon. And how can I forget Paranjyothi, who too takes his place among the sixty-three as Siruthondar?

It is hard to remember that old Aayanar and his daughter Sivakami, the heroine of the story, are entirely fictional. And so is Naganandi, the evil bikshu. Even today, when I visit the Ekamranathaswami temple in Kanchi, I can imagine Sivakami dancing 'Munnam Avanudaiya Namam Kettal', with Narasimha Pallava watching from behind a pillar. When we reached that final page in the novel, many of us wept openly. Even now, that song brings all the pent-up sorrow of Sivakami to mind.

Sivakamiyin Sabadham stands apart for yet another reason. Unlike the other two historical novels, this alone holds a mirror to society and offers a lesson to mankind. It probably came about because Kalki wrote the novel just as World War II was reaching its end. The futility of war, the colossal loss of lives, the destruction of art—these are recurring motifs in the novel. It ends on a note of unrequited love, which too is a consequence of war and conflict. At a time when yet another war is raging in the world and India is itself the stage for many smaller inter- and intra-religious conflicts, Kalki once again gains relevance with his Sivakami.

Kalki first wrote *Parthiban Kanavu* and then took up *Sivakamiyin Sabadham* as a prequel to it. Nandini Vijayaraghavan, the translator, apparently took them up in reverse order, but I guess Kalki had his way—Nandini's translation of *Parthiban Kanavu* saw the light of day first. It is not easy to translate Kalki, for he wrote in a format and idiom that was all his own, many a time engaging in a conversation with the reader. He brought his vast knowledge of world literature, Tamil poetry and philosophy into play in each of his writings. *Sivakamiyin Sabadham* is no exception. It is to the credit of Nandini that she has kept her interventions to the bare minimum and the language simple. That way we can hear Kalki, and through him the Pallavas, the Chalukyas, Sivakami, Aayanar, Naganandi and several others in their own voices.

I commend this book to all readers. May Lord Ekamranatha of Kanchi and his devotees Thirunavukkarasar and Siruthondar bless it.

Mayilai, Chennai

Sriram V.
Historian and writer

Translator's Note

Kalki R. Krishnamurthi (1899–1954), one of the most renowned Tamil writers, wrote the four-volume historical magnum opus *Sivakamiyin Sabadham* (Sivakami's Oath) as a weekly serial in his eponymous magazine, *Kalki*, between 1944 to 1946.

Kalki's expansive body of work includes editorials, short stories, film and music reviews, historical and social novels, of which *Alai Osai* (Sound of the Waves) won India's highest literary honour, the Sahitya Akademi Award. However, today he is best known for his three historical novels: *Parthiban Kanavu* (Parthiban's Dream), *Sivakamiyin Sabadham* and his swansong, *Ponniyin Selvan* (Ponni's Beloved), which was serialized between 1950 and 1954 and remains the highest-selling Tamil novel to date; it is also the inspiration for the hugely successful 2022 film directed by the acclaimed film-maker Mani Ratnam.

So popular are Kalki's works that the Tamil Nadu government nationalized them, along with those of certain other Tamil authors. This gave multiple publishers the opportunity to print his bestselling novels. Over time, certain discrepancies in the chapter titles, character names and locations crept in. My translation is based on the novel as published by projectmadurai.org.

Sivakamiyin Sabadham, to me, is the most poignant and nuanced of his three historical novels. Kalki penned *Parthiban Kanavu*, which is the sequel to *Sivakamiyin Sabadham*, before the latter was serialized. However, the plots of *Sivakamiyin Sabadham* and *Parthiban Kanavu* occurred to Kalki simultaneously. In his biography of Kalki, *Ponniyin Pudhalvar* (Ponni's Son), the journalist Sunda states that Kalki, the Tamil scholar T.K. Chidambaranatha Mudaliar and two other friends were sitting at one of the sandy, scenic beaches of Mamallapuram—present-day Mahabalipuram, the ancient Pallava port city near Chennai—on a full-moon night. It was here that a vision of 'Aayanar and Sivakami, Mahendra Pallava and Narasimha Pallava, Parthiban and Vikraman, Arulmozhi and Kundavai, Ponnan and Valli, Kannan and Kamali, and Pulikesi and Naganandi', against the backdrop of Mamallapuram during the Pallava reign, unfolded before him. This vision impelled Kalki to write *Parthiban Kanavu*, an instant hit, which was responsible for an exponential increase in his magazine's circulation. *Sivakamiyin Sabadham* followed a year later in 1944.

So why exactly is *Sivakamiyin Sabadham* so close to my heart?

Mahendra Pallava I (reigned c. 600–630 CE) withstood the invasion of the Chalukya ruler Pulakeshin II (also known as Pulikesi, reigned c. 610–642 CE), whose army was larger and better armed than the Pallava army, with mixed results. Though Pulikesi was unable to conquer the Pallava kingdom, the Chalukyas did annex certain border territories.

Narasimha Pallava I (reigned c. 630–668 CE), Mahendra Pallava's son, retaliated by invading and destroying the Chalukya capital, Vatapi (present-day Badami) and killing Pulikesi. These, along with the battles of Pullalur and Manimangalam, which Kalki so masterfully narrates, are historical occurrences. By adding fictional characters—key among whom are Aayanar, Sivakami, and Naganandi—and using the socio-political milieu of that era to explore the motivations for historical occurrences, Kalki weaves a gripping tale.

Mark Twain observed, 'History never repeats itself, but it does often rhyme.' It is apt that this translation is being published amid the Russian invasion of Ukraine that began in 2022. Fourteen centuries separate the Chalukya and Russian invasions. And yet, there lies a striking similarity—both wars demonstrate that human will triumphs over large, well-equipped armies. *Sivakamiyin Sabadham,* and to a certain extent *Parthiban Kanavu*, when juxtaposed with contemporary geopolitics, sadly remind us that humankind, notwithstanding the giant strides of progress achieved, is not yet rid of its prejudices. Readers are bound to find parallels between the religious discord described in these novels and contemporary events.

There is a fascinating conversation between Mahendra Pallava and Paranjyothi in the first volume of *Sivakamiyin Sabadham,* where the former remarks, 'A man's life is largely dependent on trees. In regions where there is lush growth of trees, rainfall is abundant. Rains fill the dams. Water levels rise in the rivers. People will be prosperous. If all the trees in a region are felled, rainfall will diminish. Famines are bound to break out.' Would the present-day aggressors have had second thoughts had they read Kalki's true-to-life descriptions of the impact of wars on the environment and humankind?

Kalki's political insights and views, a reflection of his participation in India's freedom movement and experience as a journalist covering politics, demonstrate how statecraft is a double-edged sword. His novels narrate how rulers, and by extension politicians, work for the betterment and detriment of citizens, and may educate and misinform people. In a tantalizing tête-à-tête that occurs between Naganandi and Pulikesi, the former paints a campaign amid a stalemate as a victory. Naganandi insists, 'What do you term as defeat? Who was defeated? Haven't you learnt the first lesson in statecraft yet? The lesson is that a ruler ought to never, ever acknowledge defeat. If you acknowledge your defeat, your subjects will also say so. Your foes will echo your words . . . Three key monarchs of Tamizhagam—the Cholan, Cheran and Pandian—acknowledged your supremacy and paid tribute to you on the banks of the Kaveri River . . . Just like Mahavishnu, who placed his leg on Mahabali's head, you too placed your leg on Mahendra Pallavan's head and deigned to let him live. You collected tribute from him and left Kanchi . . .'

Pulikesi points out that the Chola king had not even met him and that he did not collect tribute from Mahendra Pallava; in the novel it is Pulikesi who calls for a truce. Naganandi ought to be designated the patron saint of spin doctors for his response: 'Who is going to inquire about the details?'

Kalki's historical novels do not recast the past according to contemporary values. Aayanar telling Sivakami that it does not behove women to laugh aloud and often; the narrator stating that Sivakami, characteristic of well-bred women, looked down while entering the Pallava court ahead of her dance recital; and Narasimha Pallava opining in *Parthiban Kanavu* that women cannot be expected to be logical—these moments highlight the numerous restrictions imposed on women and society's biases against them.

Nevertheless, the women in Kalki's epics are not meek and submissive. He drew inspiration from history and mythology, and combined this with his aspirations for contemporary women to create memorable female characters. Kundavai and Valli in *Parthiban Kanavu*, Nandini, Sembiyan Maadevi and Kundavai in *Ponniyin Selvan*, and Sivakami and Kamali in *Sivakamiyin Sabadham* appear to conform to society's strictures while being decisive and fighting unarmed for the causes they believe in.

Of these glorious women, Sivakami lingers in my mind the longest. This commoner and a 'mere' dancer had the audacity to not only reciprocate the crown prince's overtures but also cross swords with an emperor and negotiate with the Chalukyas. Sivakami outshines Nandini of *Ponniyin Selvan* by accomplishing what she set out to do and refusing to allow circumstances to constrain her. Sivakami being a commoner and the novel examining the constraints and liberties that apply to civilians and royalty, distinguishes it from *Ponniyin Selvan* and *Parthiban Kanavu*, which predominantly dwell on the predicaments faced by royalty.

I owe my foray into writing and translation to Kalki and, in particular, to *Sivakamiyin Sabadham*. This was among the novels my grandmother, Vedavalli Sadagopan, would read to me during my summer holiday visits to Kumbakonam, a temple town located on the banks of the Kaveri and Arasalar. Veda Paati, as I used to call her, was an accomplished singer and violinist. She would set the poetry which appears in the novel to tune impromptu and sing as she read the novel. Reading *Sivakamiyin Sabadham* two decades later, I lived the novel as I read it, thanks to Kalki's consummate storytelling. I laughed, cried, fell in love, waged wars, committed follies, faced the consequences and emerged as a different person.

Sivakami had possessed me, unbeknownst to me. A year after I read the novel, I visited the Ekambaranathar temple at Kanchipuram, where the climax of Sivakami dancing to 'Munnam Avanudiya Namam Kettal' and Narasimha Pallava discreetly watching her unfolded before me. I shed copious tears, much to the consternation of my son, Siddharth, and the priest.

I returned to Singapore and started translating *Sivakamiyin Sabadham*. I did not know why; I did not have a plan. People I had not known from before partnered with me with equal zeal. They include Mrs Rajam Anand and Mr Narayan Anand, who translated the poetry in *Sivakamiyin Sabadham* and edited the novel. Radha Sampath proofread the translation, Rama Sundar formatted the manuscript, Namasivayam designed the publicity materials, and Suchitra Balagopal created and maintains my blog, www.litintrans.com. Special thanks to Anitha Ramkumar, who reached out to me suggesting I convert the blog to a book and introduced me to Rajam Mami and Anand Mama. I am very grateful to these people—my dear friends and most enthusiastic cheerleaders.

Translating this novel led me to meet yet another Sahitya Akademi Award winner, a writer whose work I immensely admire, the late Ashokamitran. I am deeply indebted to him for having read all four volumes of my translation and giving me feedback that improved the quality of this work. A decade after I translated *Sivakamiyin Sabadham*, it received a new lease of life. My literary agent, Suhail Mathur of the Book Bakers, introduced me to Deepthi Talwar, the commissioning editor at Penguin Random House. Deepthi commissioned the translation within a month. Thank you, Deepthi and Suhail!

I was struggling to write this translator's note for more than a month. It came together on 13 November 2022, the death anniversary of my father, A.N. Vijayaraghavan. It seems apt that words found me on the day the person who instilled the love of books in me, who engaged in long conversations as we walked down Marina Beach in Chennai every Sunday and encouraged me to voice my views, even contrarian ones, left me. This book is dedicated to you, Appa.

13 November 2022 Nandini Vijayaraghavan
Singapore

Characters

Pallava Dynasty

Mahendra Varma Pallavar	Emperor of the Pallava kingdom
Bhuvana Mahadevi	Queen consort of Mahendra Varma Pallavar
Narasimha Varma Pallavar	Mahendra Varma Pallavar's only son and the crown prince of the Pallava kingdom

Chalukya Dynasty

Satyacharya Pulikesi	Emperor of the Chalukya kingdom
Vishnuvardhanan	Pulikesi's younger brother and the king of Vengi

Other Royalty

Jayanta Varma Pandian	King of the Pandya kingdom
Durvineethan	King of Ganga Nadu

Monks

Thirunavukkarasar	A Saivite monk
Naganandi adigal	A bikshu

Commoners / civilians

Aayanar	A renowned sculptor of the Pallava kingdom
Sivakami	Aayanar's daughter and a talented danseuse
Paranjyothi	A rustic youth from Thirusengattankudi in Chola Nadu
Kalipahayar	Commander of the Pallava army
Shatrugnan	Head of the espionage force of the Pallava kingdom
Gundodharan	A Pallava spy
Kannabiran	Mahendra Varma Pallavar's charioteer
Kamali	Kannabiran's wife and Sivakami's friend
Ashwabalar	Kannabiran's father
Rudrachariar	An exponent of music and Mahendra Pallavar's music teacher
Namasivaya Vaidhyar	A renowned physician and Paranjyothi's maternal uncle
Vajrabahu	Paranjyothi's co-traveller

1

Travellers

One spring evening, two travellers were walking down the highway that traversed the banks of the Mahendra Lake, towards Kancheepuram. One, a big-built six-footer, was a bikshu clad in ochre robes. His body was parched and hard either due to severe penances or due to harsh activities. His face did not evoke any feeling of love or devotion; instead, it instilled a sense of fear. The other traveller was an eighteen-year-old, well-built and good-looking youth. As both of them had covered a great distance by foot, they appeared tired.

'How far is the capital?' enquired the youth.

'There,' said the bikshu. Turrets of mansions were visible amidst the thick foliage in the direction he indicated.

The young traveller gazed at this sight intently for some time. He then asked the bikshu, 'Will it take a nazhigai to reach there?'

'Yes. It should take that much time.'

'In that case, I will rest for some time and then come. Please go ahead if you are in a hurry,' said the youth, keeping his bundle and staff down. He sat down facing the lake. The bikshu sat next to him, facing the west.

In the horizon, the golden-hued sun was shining bright like Tirumal's discus. Its rays that spread across the sky gave it a red hue, like bloodshed in a battlefield. Clouds that were dispersed across the sky seemed to be on fire. Parts of the crystal-clear waters of the Mahendra Lake glittered like molten gold in the setting sun.

But the northern side of the expansive lake presented a very different picture. The shadow of the small hills that stood on the banks of the lake fell on the waters, giving it a blue-black hue. Small flocks of white cranes that stood on one foot in a meditative posture offered a stark contrast to the dark waters. Words are inadequate to describe the beauty of the sight offered by a flock taking to flight suddenly. The white cranes flying against the backdrop of the blue-black waters, dark sky and lush green hills would enthrall everyone. The spiritually inclined would, however, become rapturous.

The youth, who observed this sight, muttered to himself, 'It is not appropriate to call this massive water body Mahendra Lake. It should be called Mahendra Ocean.'

The bikshu replied as he got up, 'The water level in the Mahendra Lake has now receded. You will be stunned when you see the lake overflowing during Aipasi and Karthigai, after the monsoons.'

'Are you leaving, swami?' asked the youth.

'Yes, Paranjyothi. You probably prefer not to accompany me,' said the bikshu as he started walking. The youth, whose name was Paranjyothi, picked up his staff and bundle and followed the bikshu.

There was a lot of traffic on the highway. Carts were transporting travellers, paddy and hay. On the other side of the highway, paddy fields were ready for harvest. Labourers were bundling the paddy already harvested. The fragrance of freshly harvested paddy and hay emanated from the fields.

There was a picturesque village down the road. As soon as one neared it, the fragrance of jasmine flowers enveloped the area. It was not just the nose but the entire body that relished the fragrance.

The youth let out an appreciative sigh. Vast flower gardens met his eye. Jasmine flowers adorned the bushes like stars in the sky. Fields filled with golden chrysanthemums dotted this white landscape.

'How will all these flowers be used?' wondered the youth.

'Some of these will be offered to the gods in the temples, while the rest will adorn the women of Kanchi . . . Look!' said the bikshu and suddenly stopped.

A snake slithered across the road into the garden, and disappeared. 'The fragrance of these jasmines attracts the snakes,' said the bikshu.

When the snake was out of sight, both resumed walking. They were silent for some time. Paranjyothi then burst out laughing. 'What prompted you to laugh?' enquired the bikshu.

Paranjyothi was silent for some time and then said, 'Adigal, this afternoon you saved me by killing a snake. Aren't you a bikshu? The thought of you engaging in violence made me laugh.'

'One can kill even a calf in self-defence,' said the bikshu.

'But the snake was about to bite me and not you,' said Paranjyothi in a mocking voice.

'Shouldn't I protect my disciple?' asked the bikshu.

'Disciple? Who are you referring to?'

'You once saved my life. My act was out of gratitude . . .'

'When did I save your life?'

'Three hundred years ago . . .'

'What!'

'In a previous birth.'

'Oh! You're a seer who is aware of the past, present and the future. Please forgive me.'

The bikshu walked silently.

Paranjyothi enquired, 'Swami, can you predict the future?'

'Shall I tell you of a future occurrence?'

'Please tell me.'

'This country will face a huge war.'

'War?'

'Yes, a terrible war. Blood will flow in the Palar River. The Mahendra Lake will be filled with blood.'

'Aiyya, that scares me. That's enough.'

After some time, Paranjyothi said, 'The affairs of the state do not concern me. If you know something about my future, please tell me.'

'Tonight you will get into trouble.'

'Shiva Shiva! Can't you say something good?'

'By Lord Buddha's grace, you will overcome the difficulty.'

'I am a Saivite. Will Lord Buddha bless me?'

'Lord Buddha's kindness is boundless.'

'Who is walking towards us?' asked Paranjyothi.

In the dim twilight, a wondrous figure was approaching them.

'Isn't it evident? A Digambar Jain monk is coming,' said the bikshu.

'Are Jain monks still here?' enquired Paranjyothi.

'Most of them have left for the Pandya kingdom. The rest are leaving.'

The Jain monk approached them. Unlike the bikshu, he was short and squat. He was wearing just a loincloth. In one hand he was carrying a kamandalam, a fan made of peacock feathers in the other and a small mat under his arm.

As he came near, the bikshu said, 'Buddham saranam gacchami.'

The Jain monk said, 'Hail the feet of Lord Mahaveera.'

'Aiyya, where are you going in this darkness?' asked the bikshu.

The Jain monk responded, 'Ah! I have no work in this anger-filled land. Thondai Mandalam has become a graveyard in which Shiva dances. I am leaving for the Pandya kingdom.'

'Is there any important event today?' enquired the bikshu.

'Yes, the entrance to the fort is going to be sealed,' said the Jain monk as he resumed walking.

'At one time, the Jains were very powerful in the Pallava kingdom. King Mahendra Pallavar conformed to the Jains' wishes. But now . . .' the bikshu stopped.

'What about now?' asked Paranjyothi.

'Nowadays the Saivites and Vaishnavites have a lot of clout.'

'Oh! The Jain monk was mentioning that the gates of the fort are going to be closed. What was he referring to?' Paranjyothi asked.

'Look there!' said the bikshu.

As they turned a corner, the western side of the Kanchi Fort became visible. The massive gates were sealed.

2

Capital

There was a large moat encircling the walls of the fort. It was about a hundred feet wide and quite deep. The water in the moat was blue-green.

The highway down which our travellers came forked into two near the moat. One branch of the highway turned right and the other ran adjacent to the moat. Travellers and carts which came down the highway turned either left or right and continued their journey. The narrow wooden bridge across the moat led to the gates of the fort. The bikshu gestured to Paranjyothi to follow him as he walked across the bridge. Paranjyothi complied.

'Why is the bridge so narrow? How will vehicles enter the fort?' asked Paranjyothi.

'They cannot enter through this gate. The bridges to the northern and eastern gates are wide. Even elephants can walk across those bridges,' said the bikshu. They crossed the bridge and reached the entrance of the fort. A gong was suspended there, with a stick beside it. The bikshu hit the gong with the stick.

A man looked out from the higher storey of the fort and asked, 'Who's that?'

As it was dark, one could not recognize his face. 'It's me, Marudappa,' said the bikshu.

'Is that you, adigal! I will come right away,' said the man and disappeared.

Sometime later, the clicking sound of bolts was heard and the fort door opened wide enough to let just one person in. The bikshu entered the fort and then pulled Paranjyothi inside. The door was then shut.

Paranjyothi looked towards the city as soon as he stepped in. Kanchi was illuminated by bright lamps. The din of thousands of people talking could be heard. As Paranjyothi had never been in a big city until now, he was astounded.

The bikshu asked the guard who opened the door, 'Marudappa, why does the city seem subdued? Why were the fort gates shut so early? Is there any news?'

'I do not know the exact reason. The city was quite festive this morning . . .'

As Marudappan was talking, the bikshu interrupted to ask, 'Why?'

'Don't you know? Today Sivakami's Bharatanatyam arangetram was to be held at the emperor's court. So, people were exuberant.'

'Which Sivakami are you referring to?' asked the bikshu.

'Aayanar's daughter, Sivakami.'

Paranjyothi, who had not been attentive thus far asked, 'Who? Aayanar, the sculptor?'

'Yes,' responded the guard, looking at Paranjyothi intently. 'Adigal, who is this boy?' he asked the bikshu.

'He is my disciple; you tell me further.'

'As the arangetram was underway, emissaries came with some important news. The chakravarthy left the court immediately. He did not return. The kumara chakravarthy and ministers also left. The arangetram ended abruptly. I received orders to seal the fort gates at sunset. What can it be, aiyya? Will there be a war soon? But who on earth is strong enough to wage a war against the chakravarthy of Kanchi?' said Marudappan.

'Don't say that, Marudappa. One never knows what the future holds, even for emperors. But why do we need to discuss these things. How is your son?' asked the bikshu.

'He is fine by your grace, swami,' said Marudappan.

Marudappan's son had once been bitten by a snake. The chances of his survival were slim, but the bikshu had saved him by administering medicines. This was the reason for Maruddapan's gratitude and devotion to the bikshu.

'It is not because of me, Marudappa. It is by Lord Buddha's grace . . . I shall leave now,' said the bikshu and moved on. Paranjyothi followed him.

'Adigal, how did he let you enter, despite orders to seal the fort gates?' Paranjyothi asked.

'It is due to the ochre robes I'm wearing,' said the bikshu.

'I didn't know that bikshus were honored in the Pallava kingdom. But why do the Jains . . . ?'

'Jains interfered with the affairs of the state. We do not get involved in politics. In fact, we do not even meet people from the ruling dynasty. Anyway, what are your plans? Do you want to come with me to the viharam?'

'No, swami. I am headed to Navukkarasar's monastery. My mother insisted that I stay nowhere but there.'

'In that case, we have to part ways here.'

'Swami, do you know where Navukkarasar's monastery is? How do I get there?' Paranjyothi asked.

'It is close to the Ekambareshwar temple. Look at the temple tower there.'

Paranjyothi looked around. Several temple towers dotted the landscape of this large city. During the time of this story, almost one thousand three hundred and twenty years ago, the towers of temples in Tamil Nadu were not as high as they are now. Towers were constructed above the temple's sanctum sanctorum. Moreover, temple towers, turrets of Jain schools and palace roofs were all similar.

'There are towers everywhere. Which one are you referring to?' asked Paranjyothi.

'It is difficult to point out from here. You go down this street and then enquire. Navukkarasar's monastery is close to the temple's sanctum. Careful, my boy. These are dangerous times.' So saying, the bikshu went down another road.

The young traveller walked in the direction shown by the bikshu. In those times, Kanchi was amongst the most prominent cities in Dakshina Bharata. Every street in the city was wide enough for chariots to pass. Houses were large. Stone pillars were erected across the city. Large earthen lamps placed on these pillars burned brightly. The marketplace was filled with produce from Kashi to Kanyakumari. Shops selling fruits, flowers, confectionery, grains and precious gems were in the marketplace.

Paranjyothi was filled with boundless amazement as he walked down these streets. He heard people discussing the abrupt end of Sivakami's arangetram and the fort being sealed. Periodically, he asked a passer-by, 'Where is the Ekambareshwarar temple?' They guided him. But he took time to reach the temple as he was immersed in the novel sights and sounds of the city and was in no hurry.

As he was strolling down the streets, he suddenly heard a lot of noise and commotion. People frantically dispersed in all directions. 'The temple elephant is running amok. Flee! Flee!' they warned. The sounds of children crying, women screaming, doors of houses being hurriedly shut, cows mooing and carts hurriedly moving caused indescribable confusion.

Paranjyothi was stunned for a moment. He was unable to decide whether he should also run and, if so, in which direction. He observed the incidents unfolding before him. Ahead of him, there was a palanquin. A stunningly beautiful young woman and an old man who seemed to be her father were seated in the palanquin. The palanquin bearers, hearing the commotion behind them, set the palanquin down on the road and fled. Simultaneously, he could hear from behind the mad elephant running towards him at a speed that caused the ground to vibrate.

Paranjyothi stood indecisively for a moment. The next moment he opened his bundle quickly and resolutely. He took out the tip of a spear from inside and attached it to the staff he was carrying. By the time he held the spear in his right hand, the elephant had come close.

Paranjyothi hurled the spear at the elephant with all his might. The spear hit the elephant near the left eye, piercing its thick hide as it struck deep. It let out a terrible cry, removed the spear with its trunk and stamped it under its foot. Then it turned towards the youth who had flung the spear.

Paranjyothi knew the consequences of attacking a mad elephant. So, he started running quickly in the direction opposite to where the palanquin was. By the time the elephant moved its gigantic body around, he had covered a long distance. As he was running, he turned around and looked.

The elephant was chasing him. Immediately, he ran down a by-lane without looking back. He again reached a wide road and saw five to six elephants manned by mahouts approaching the spot rapidly. He stood at the corner of the street. He guessed that these elephants were being sent to tame the mad elephant and started walking slowly.

Paranjyothi became conscious of his body only then. His heart was beating rapidly. He was drenched in sweat. As he had been walking the whole day, he was already tired and the running made him even more exhausted. His feet slackened. His body shivered due to the excitement. He felt incapable of walking further and wanted to sit down to relax for some time. He sat on a stone platform erected on the roadside.

The full moon was glowing brightly in the sky. The gentle breeze that was blowing helped him relax. As he recovered, he started thinking, 'What was the purpose of my visit? Why did I get involved in this adventure? What motivated me to hurl the spear at the mad elephant? What would have been the consequences had the elephant caught up with me? I would have never again seen my mother, who loves me more dearly than her own life, again.'

Paranjyothi recollected the faces of the young woman and the old man seated in the palanquin. He resolved that he had hurled the spear at the mad elephant to protect them. 'Who could they have been? Was she Sivakami, whose arangetram people said ended midway? Was the elderly gentleman Aayanar?' Paranjyothi, thinking thus, lay down on the stone platform. His eyelids closed involuntarily. Nitra Devi embraced him gently in her soft arms.

3

Pampered Child

Sengattankudi, a prosperous village in eastern Chola Nadu, lay in the fertile Ponni delta region. Paranjyothi, a native to this village, was born in a noble family that was conferred with the title 'Mamathirar'. When the entire Chola kingdom was under the Uraiyur Cholas, Paranjyothi's ancestors were commanders in the army. As the Chola dynasty became weak and the Pallavas gained supremacy, the Mamathirars lost their pre-eminent position in society. The Mamathirars of the generations immediately preceding Parajyothi's had given up war and border defence, and were engaged in agriculture.

Paranjyothi had lost his father at an early age and was pampered by his mother. Neighbours said that he was a wicked ruffian. He loved to fight. He had a natural flair for making weapons. The bravery and valour of the Mamathirars of yore coursed through Paranjyothi's veins. Within a short time, he attained proficiency in cane fight, sword fight, wrestling and wielding the spear.

Paranjyothi's mother, Vadivazhagi Ammai, loved her son more dearly than her own life. Nevertheless, Paranjyothi's boisterous antics concerned her. She was born in a family that was devoted to Lord Shiva and was well versed in the arts. Her brother, Namasivaya Vaidhyar, was a prominent doctor in Thiruvengadu. He was an ardent devotee of Lord Shiva, proficient in Tamil and also well versed in Sanskrit.

His eldest daughter was Umayal. This beautiful girl was virtuous, well educated and deeply devoted to Lord Shiva. Paranjyothi's mother secretly desired that Paranjyothi marry Umayal. But she was doubtful if her wish would be fulfilled. Would a multifaceted person like her brother consent to the marriage of his dear daughter with a ruffian like Paranjyothi?

Vadivazhagi Ammai tried her best to educate Paranjyothi. But all those teachers who had attempted to educate Paranjyothi had failed. None of them were able to teach Paranjyothi for a long time. Each one of them, after trying for some time, had told his mother, 'Thaye, your son is very intelligent. If he applies his mind to it, he can understand anything in the first instance. But, we need to strive hard to get him to concentrate. We do not have the wherewithal to teach him,' and had left. A couple of teachers who had used the cane left without informing Paranjyothi's mother.

These issues worried Vadivazhagi Ammai a lot. One year, Paranjyothi and Vadivazhagi Ammai went to Thiruvengadu for the Pongal festival. Paranjyothi saw Umayal there. He heard that Umayal's family was looking for a groom for her. He heard his uncle and his mother discuss his activities in a concerned manner and understood the situation.

After they returned to Sengattankudi from Thiruvengadu, one day, Vadivazhagi Ammai lay on the floor shedding tears. Paranjyothi, who returned home after strolling outside, saw his mother weeping and sat next to her. He did not enquire why she was weeping. He did not console her.

'Mother, you should not disagree with what I am about to say,' he said.

His mother wiped her tears and asked, 'What is it, my dear?'

When he said, 'I am going to Kanchi,' she got up with a start.

'Why?' she asked.

'To educate myself, mother. I regret being uneducated and wasting my time all these years,' said Paranjyothi.

His mother shed tears of joy and sorrow at the same time. 'Why do you have to go to Kanchi to educate yourself? Can't you study here?' she asked.

'As long as I am here, I will not study. People say that one has to go to Kanchi to get quality education. Apparently, Kanchi has the best academies and art schools in the whole of the Bharata Kanda. I have inquired before reaching this conclusion, mother,' said Paranjyothi.

What Paranjyothi said was true. In those days, Kanchi was the abode of Goddess Saraswati. The city was filled with schools and monasteries which imparted knowledge of the Vedas, Sanskrit, Tamil, Buddhism and Jainism. Art schools which taught painting, sculpture and music were also located there.

Besides, a few years ago, an incident that enthused all the people in Tamil Nadu occurred in Kanchi. By the grace of Thirunavukkarasar, the brave and wise Chakravarthy Mahendra Varmar had converted to Saivism from Jainism. Navukkarasar was christened 'Marul Neekiyar'. He assumed the name 'Dharmasena' and was renowned amongst Jain monks. Later, he became a Saivite, influenced by his sister, Thilakavathi. From then on, he composed poetry in mellifluous Tamil that infused listeners with Shiva bhakti. Listening to these divine songs, Chakravarthy Mahendra Varmar said,

'I rule the nation while you rule the spoken word.'* Thus praising Marul Neekiyar, Chakravarthy Mahendra Varmar embraced Saivism. News of this incident spread across Tamil Nadu and people spoke of this with wonder. At the request of Mahendra Varmar, Thirunavukkarasar established a monastery which became renowned for imparting Tamil and devotional music education in Kanchi. Paranjyothi heard of these incidents and told his mother that he was going to Kanchi to educate himself.

Though the thought of being separated from her only son made Vadivazhagi Ammai very sad, Paranjyothi's resolve to educate himself gave her boundless happiness. After obtaining his mother's consent, Paranjyothi said, 'Mother, you should speak to uncle and ensure that Umayal is not married till I return.' When she became aware of her son's desire, Vadivazhagi Ammai shed tears of joy.

Paranjyothi's uncle was also extremely happy when he came to know of his intentions. As Namasivaya Vaidhyar shared a cordial relationship with Thirunavukkarasar, he promised to send a message to the monk. The uncle also said that he would send a message to his old friend Aayanar to teach Paranjyothi an art. Sensing his nephew's unstated desire, Namasivaya Vaidhyar promised to get Umayal married to Paranjyothi once he completed his education.

On an auspicious day and time, Paranjyothi sought the blessings of his mother and uncle, took leave from the rest of his family and proceeded to Kanchi. Before leaving, his uncle advised him as follows, 'Paranjyothi, when you are travelling a long distance, it is only fair that you carry a spear. But keep the spear as a safety measure only for the journey. Once you reach Kanchi, fling it away. All your attention must then be focused on education.'

---

* 'Thirunavukkarasar' means 'ruler of the tongue' in Tamil.

4

God Saved Us

The elderly man and the young woman in the palanquin watched the youth hurling the spear with lightning speed at the mad elephant and the elephant chasing him in retaliation. Amazed by his foresight and courage, they hoped no danger would befall him. They hurriedly stepped out of the palanquin as they were eager to know what had happened to him. At that moment, there was no human movement on that wide road; it was deserted.

The elderly man embraced the young girl and asked her affectionately, 'Are you afraid, Sivakami?'

'Not at all, appa. I am not scared,' she said. She then asked, 'What would have happened to us, had that youth not distracted the elephant?'

'The palanquin would have been smashed to smithereens,' replied her father. 'That is why the bearers set the palanquin down and fled. We too could have sought refuge in a neighbouring house. But we were in grave danger,' said the elderly man.

People who had fled from the street slowly returned one by one. As everyone started discussing the recent events, the street which had previously been silent reverberated with the noise of human conversation. They said, 'Isn't that Aayanar and his daughter? Thank God for saving them. 'It was God who came in the form of that youth and saved them.

Aayanar and his daughter wondered, 'Who is that youth? What happened to him?' But nobody was aware of the young man's identity or whereabouts.

Aayanar went close to the place where the elephant had last stood. He picked up the spear that had been crushed by the elephant, tied up Paranjyothi's bundle that lay open some distance away and returned to the palanquin. Sivakami looked at the crushed spear with amazement.

'Sivakami, it is pointless to continue standing here. Let's go. All details will be known tomorrow,' said Aayanar. As father and daughter were about to enter the palanquin, they heard the sound of horses rapidly approaching. They were perplexed.

As the horses stopped near the palanquin, people moved away deferentially. 'Long live Mahendra Varma Pallavar! Long live the chakravarthy of the three realms! Long live the virtuous king! Long live Kumara Chakravarthy Mamallar!'

When Aayanar and Sivakami realized that the people who had come riding on the white horses were the chakravarthy, Mahendra Varma Pallavar and his only son, Narasimha Varma, they were amazed. Sivakami bashfully stood behind Aayanar. She gazed at the kumara chakravarthy, who followed the chakravarthy, with her wide eyes.

'Aayanar, what happened? What I heard was disastrous.' So saying, Mahendra Varmar alighted from the horse.

'By the grace of Lord Ekambarar, no mishap occurred, prabhu,' said Aayanar.

'Was Sivakami very frightened?' asked the chakravarthy.

'Sivakami was not frightened. She found the incident entertaining.' So saying, Aayanar shot a loving glance at Sivakami.

The chakravarthy looked at Sivakami affectionately and asked, 'Sivakami, why are you looking down? Are you angry that I left in the middle of your arangetram?'

A shy smile blossomed on Sivakami's face. She remained silent. Then Aayanar said, 'Oh Pallava Chakravarthy! Doesn't Sivakami know? You must have left because you had an extremely important task to attend . . .'

'Yes, Aayanar, it was an extremely important task. I will tell you about it later. When the discussions with the ministers' council were over, I enquired about you. I was informed that you had left. Where are you going in such a hurry?' asked the chakravarthy.

'Only if we reach home tonight can I commence working in the morning. I do not want to waste even a single day, prabhu!'

'Yes, you will not be able to refrain from your divine art for even a day. Do you still intend returning home tonight?'

'Yes, my lord. The moon shines so bright that it looks like day. It is convenient to return tonight.'

'Looking at the milky-white moon, I too feel like accompanying you. But that is not possible. I will come tomorrow or the day after.' So saying, the chakravarthy looked around.

Narasimha Varmar, alighting skilfully from his white horse, came up to the chakravarthy and asked, 'Appa, did you enquire about the youth who hurled the spear at the elephant?'

He then asked Aayanar, 'Who was he? Where did he go? Do you know anything?'

'I don't know anything. He disappeared in a flash as soon as he hurled the spear and thus saved himself. He seemed to have come from another country,' said Aayanar.

As the kumara chakravarthy was talking to Aayanar, his gaze was fixed on Sivakami, who still stood behind Aayanar. Sivakami, who had been looking at Narasimha Varmar intently when he was seated on the horse, did not even look in his direction. She was staring at the ground. The broken spear that had slipped from her hand lay on the ground. Narasimha Varmar, who saw it, approached her, asking, 'Sivakami, what is this?' Sivakami took a step back, picked up the broken spear and held it towards him. As Narasimha Varmar took it, his fingers must have touched Sivakami's. One could guess it from the way they moved apart as though a scorpion had stung them.

Narasimha Varmar controlled his excitement and asked Aayanar, 'Wasn't this the spear that saved you from the mad elephant?'

'Yes, Pallava kumara,' replied Aayanar.

As he was about to say something, Mamallar looked at his father and said, 'Appa! We must definitely trace the person who wielded this spear. Had he not acted valorously, wouldn't we have lost the greatest sculptor of the Pallava kingdom?'

To which the chakravarthy responded, 'We wouldn't have just lost the greatest sculptor but also the most renowned goddess of art. We should find that hero. Let them go. It is already late.' He then turned to Sivakami and said, 'My child! Your dance was wonderful today. But I was unable to watch it completely.' He then told Aayanar, 'Aayanar, I need to discuss a lot of things with you. I will soon come to Mamallapuram. But now, please go home safely.'

The chakravarthy, who realized that Aayanar and Sivakami would not enter the palanquin as long as he was there, quickly mounted his horse. Narasimha Varmar followed suit. Before leaving, Mahendra Varmar gestured to one of the soldiers behind him. 'Detain any youth who has come from outside and produce him at the palace tomorrow morning. Communicate this order to the head of the city's security immediately,' he ordered.

As soon as the chakravarthy and the kumara chakravarthy left, Aayanar and Sivakami sat in their palanquin. Surrounded by guards, the palanquin reached the eastern gates of the fort.

5

Bad Omen

Paranjyothi had hardly closed his eyes, leaning against the stone platform, when he heard some voices and woke up with a start.

'It is said that a temple elephant running amok is a bad omen!'

'Yes, the country is going to face danger.'

'How did the elephant go mad?'

'Who knows? Apparently, an outsider hurled a spear at the elephant. That's why the elephant ran amok.'

'Aayanar and his daughter escaping was like rebirth for them.'

'As if it was not enough that the arangetram was interrupted midway, they also had to face danger.'

Paranjyothi did not hear beyond this. His heart skipped a beat when he heard that the reason for the elephant running amok was attributed to his hurling the spear. He then recollected something else. He had abandoned the bundle he was carrying on the road when he fled from the elephant. The bundle contained epistles addressed to Navukkarasar and Aayanar, his clothes and a little money. He would definitely have to find it. Would he be able to find it at the place where he had left it? How would he be able to find the place where he had left the bundle when he did not know his way around the city?

Paranjyothi got down from the stone platform, tried to guess the road down which he had come running and started walking in that direction. By then, human traffic on the roads had reduced. The doors of houses were shut. Street lights were extinguished. Fortunately, the full moon was showering its milky-white glow. Paranjyothi keenly observed his surroundings in the moonlight, as he walked a long distance.

As it was late night, the streets were silent. Observing the position of the moon in the sky, Paranjyothi realized it was midnight. His legs refused to move further. He felt like lying down somewhere. It was pointless looking for his bundle. He just wanted to go to Navukkarasar's monastery.

But, how did one reach there? There was no one to ask for directions. Paranjyothi felt odd wandering desolately in a city inhabited by lakhs of people. He wondered if he would have to wander all night like this. In a city with thousands of mansions, halls and houses, wasn't there a place for him to stay in the night? Fortunately, he saw some people coming and could hear their voices. He thought he could to ask them for directions.

Two people were walking down a street corner, talking to each other. They seemed to be the city guards. When they saw Paranjyothi, they stopped.

'Who are you, boy? Where are you going at this time of the night?' asked one of them.

'I am from outside this city, aiyya . . .'

As Paranjyothi was answering them, the man who spoke first asked, 'From outside? Which place are you from?'

'The Chola kingdom . . .'

'Uraiyur?'

'No, aiyya. From the eastern part of the Chola kingdom, a village called Sengattankudi. I reached Kanchi this evening.'

'Is that so? Why did you come here?'

'To learn Tamil at Navukkarasar's monastery.'

'Then why are you wandering around in the middle of the night?'

'I do not know where the monastery is. I have been searching for it since evening.'

The two guards smiled mockingly. One of them asked, 'Do you necessarily have to go to Navukkarasar's monastery?'

'Yes, aiyya!'

'We are going in that direction. If you come with us, we will leave you there.'

Paranjyothi thanked them and followed them. In a short time, they reached the entrance of a building surrounded by high compound walls.

'Is this the monastery?' Paranjyothi asked.

'Yes. Doesn't this look like a monastery?'

In truth, Paranjyothi did not believe that the building was a monastery. There was no temple close by. The high walls and the big lock that secured the front doors aroused an indescribable suspicion.

One of the guards who accompanied him said something to the guard at the entrance. Immediately, the door was unlocked and opened.

'Come, boy!'

Paranjyothi's heart was beating wildly as he entered the building. They took him down a narrow lane flanked by high walls on both sides. They stopped and opened the doors of a room.

'You lie down here. Everyone in the monastery is asleep. We will come back in the morning,' said one guard.

Paranjyothi looked into the dark room. There was some hay and a bamboo mat. In one corner, there was an earthen pot. He turned around to the guards and asked, 'This is the monastery, isn't it?'

'Yes, boy. Why the doubt?'

'If you don't want to stay here, you may leave,' said one guard.

Paranjyothi was so tired that he wanted to just lie down somewhere. 'No, I will lie down here,' he said as he entered the room.

One of the guards who had brought him there said, 'Boy, this is a monastery too. Not Navukkarasar's monastery, but the Chakravarthy Mahendra Varmar's monastery.' So saying, he shut the door. The sound of the door being locked was heard.

6

Mysterious Rope

As he lay on the mat in the dark room of the prison complex, Paranjyothi recollected his uncle's advice. As soon as he had reached Kanchi, he had flung the spear away. But that mischievous spear had found its mark in the mad elephant. Paranjyothi was amused when he realized that he had landed in jail because of this incident.

What would his mother and uncle think if they came to know that he had spent the very first night after coming to Kanchi in prison? How would Umayal, whose eyes were filled with concern and tears as he was leaving for Kanchi, feel?

If he related this incident on returning to his village after learning Tamil and sculpture, it was quite possible that people would not believe him. Had someone predicted in the afternoon what he would go through in the evening, would he have believed it?

Suddenly, Paranjyothi remembered something. What had that bikshu said? Hadn't he said Paranjyothi would face difficulty tonight? That had come true. Was he truly a seer?

Paranjyothi laughed to himself when he thought of how he had met the bikshu. After walking all morning, he realized that Kanchi was about one kadu away. He lay down under a tree by the side of the road to rest. He had placed his bundle under his head and his spear next to him.

Thinking that there may be poisonous creatures and wild animals in the vicinity, Paranjyothi did not sleep. He alternated between closing his eyes for some time and waking up whenever he heard some noise.

After some time, he saw a bikshu walking along the road. His uncle and mother had insisted that he ought not to socialize with Buddhists and Jains and that he should steer clear of them.

So, when he observed the bikshu from a distance, he closed his eyes. He decided to pretend to be asleep till the ascetic had passed by him and had walked a considerable distance. After some time, he sensed someone standing next to him, looking at him intently. He slowly opened his eyes.

Paranjyothi was a courageous youth. But when he opened his eyes, he trembled at the sight before him. The bikshu, whom he had seen at a distance, was standing next to him and was staring at him. The bikshu's appearance instilled fear in him. In fact, he felt more disgust than fear at the sight of the snake hanging upside down from the bikshu's hand. The bikshu was holding the snake by its tail.

It was a five-foot-long cobra, but it was dead. It was bleeding. Paranjyothi got up exclaiming, 'Aiyya! What kind of a joke is this? Why are you holding a dead snake? Throw it away!'

'My son! How can you sleep alone in this forest area? By now, this cobra would have bitten you. Luckily I came and killed this snake and you were saved.' So saying, the bikshu flung the snake away.

Paranjyothi suppressed a smile and said, 'Is that so, aiyya? I am my mother's only child. My mother would be very grateful to you for having saved me.'

He then took his bundle and spear and stood up. He asked, 'What is your name, aiyya? If I have to tell my mother about you . . .'

The bikshu interrupted saying, 'People call me Naganandi. My son, where are you going?'

As soon as Paranjyothi said, 'I am going to Kanchi,' the bikshu said, 'I am going there too. I will have company for the journey. Come, let's go.'

Lying down in the dark room, Paranjyothi thought, 'The name Naganandi is so appropriate for that bikshu. His face is reminiscent of a cobra.'

Paranjyothi did not know if that bikshu was truly able to see into the future or if his predictions were a fluke. But the first of his predictions had come true. He realized that he was ensnared in a difficult situation. Would his other prediction also come true? He had also said, 'By Lord Buddha's grace, you will overcome the difficulty.' Paranjyothi hoped it would also come true.

Paranjyothi thought that, irrespective of whether his difficulty was resolved immediately or after some time, it would have to be through Lord Shiva's kindness and not Lord Buddha's grace. Truly, Paranjyothi was not very concerned about his situation. It was obvious that he had not committed any mistake and had performed a momentous task. He firmly believed that he had been erroneously imprisoned and that he would be released once the truth was known.

So, it was right to sleep well that night. But why wasn't he able to sleep? Oh, it was all because of his stomach. He hadn't had dinner. His stomach was grumbling. That was why he was unable to sleep. The city of Kanchi starves its guests who have travelled a long distance, he thought. It was only because he met that bikshu that he was starving.

As Paranjyothi was thinking along these lines, a change in the room caught his attention. There was light streaming into the room, which had been dark till then. A surprised Paranjyothi looked up to ascertain the cause for this change. Moonlight was streaming into the room through a small hole in the roof.

Paranjyothi was surprised at the appearance of the hole, which had not existed till some time ago. 'No, no! The hole must have always been there. The moon must have just moved above the hole.' This thought reassured Paranjyothi. The full moon had transformed the area outside the prison into a beautiful dream world. The moon rays were teasingly streaming into the prison to make him aware of the beauty outside, kindling his envy.

Ah! What is this? The moonlight that was streaming in seemed to be brighter. It seemed as though the hole was becoming bigger. The aperture which had not been big enough to let a hand in was now large enough for a human to pass through. Was this Indra's magic or Mahendra's magic? Kanchi, which was ruled by Mahendra chakravarthy, seemed to be a mysterious city!

Oh! What is this disaster? It seemed as though Paranjyothi's breath would stop for a moment. No, it was not a snake slithering through the hole. When he realized that it was just a rope, he relaxed. Ever since the bikshu had frightened him with a dead snake, even a rope seemed to be a snake to him.

Paranjyothi now understood the mystery of the aperture on the roof. Someone had intentionally made a hole in the roof and let a rope in. Why? Why else would they have done it except to help him escape? But in a city where he knew no one, who could be so concerned about him? How did they come to know that he was imprisoned?

Gradually, the rope was within Paranjyothi's reach. Soon, it descended further and touched the floor. Then, the rope oscillated to and fro. There was no doubt that the person who had let the rope in was shaking it. Why? Was he indicating to Paranjyothi to climb the rope? It must be so.

Paranjyothi was not sure if he should accept the unanticipated assistance. He thought for a moment that he should not accept it. He did not know what difficulty he would have to face as a result of accepting this assistance. He was also eager to know who was taking so much trouble to save him. But there was also another important aspect, and that was hunger!

Paranjyothi held the rope firmly and pulled it. It was fastened tightly at the top. It was evident that the rope could bear his weight. He immediately started climbing the rope.

7

Nila Muttram*

After taking leave of Aayanar and Sivakami, Mahendra chakravarthy and Mamallar rode swiftly back to the palace. Seeing them, the palace guards cheered, 'Long live Chakravarthy Mahendra Varmar! Long live the brave warrior, Mamallar!' and made way for them. The neighing of horses that stood in rows could be heard along with the cheering of the guards.

Soldiers were assembled in rows at the nila muttram located within the palace adjoining the front entrance. These soldiers too cheered the chakravarthy and the kumara chakravarthy. One person who stood ahead of all the soldiers approached Mahendra chakravarthy and Mamallar courteously. The chakravarthy asked him, 'Commander! Have you instructed all the emissaries? Are they ready to leave?'

---

*Loosely translated as 'moonlight courtyard'.

'Yes, my lord! I have informed everyone. They are aware of their respective destinations. All are ready to leave and are waiting for your orders,' said the commander.

The chakravarthy told Narasimha Varmar, 'My child! Your mother must be worried. Please inform her of the news. Both of you have your dinner and go to the terrace. I will join you there once I'm done with the emissaries.'

As the chakravarthy had been practising Jainism for a long time, he abstained from dinner. Even after embracing Saivism, he did not resume the habit of partaking dinner.

'Yes, father. I shall go right away. But do we have to wait till all the forces reach Kanchi? Can't we proceed to the war front with the forces that are ready?'

The chakravarthy smilingly said, 'We will think about that, my child. You go now and meet your mother.'

After Mamallar left, Mahendra Varmar spoke to Kalipahayar, the commander. 'Kalipahayar, this is the news to be conveyed to the emissaries. In every district of the Pallava and Chola kingdoms, a force of one thousand soldiers needs to be mobilized. This army should be ready to leave for the battlefield on receipt of further instructions. Do you understand what I say?'

'Yes, prabhu!'

'Have necessary arrangements been made to secure the fort?'

'I have passed orders not to let anyone but ascetics inside the fort without enquiries. I have asked the guards to monitor those who leave the fort. Any suspect in the city will be imprisoned.'

'Have the walls of the fort been checked for faults? Commander, the Pallava kingdom will flourish only if the Kanchi fort is secure.'

'Lakhs of warriors from Kaveri to Krishna will safeguard the Pallava kingdom, prabhu.'

'True, but they cannot fight with bare hands. Where are the spears and swords for the lakhs of warriors?' asked the chakravarthy.

Commander Kalipahayar remained silent.

'It seems as though people in the eastern part of the Chola kingdom make good swords and spears. Did you see the spear that was hurled at the elephant?'

'No, prabhu.'

'It is with Narasimhar. The word "Mamathirar" is inscribed on it. Isn't the title "Mamathirar" native to the eastern part of the Chola kingdom?'

'Yes, my lord.'

'The person who wielded the spear must be native to the eastern region of Chola Nadu. If we had a thousand such soldiers, there would be no concern about the security of this fort.'

'There are thousands of warriors who wield the spear in the Pallava army, prabhu!'

'The person who wielded the spear is a rare breed. It is essential to find him.'

The commander remained silent.

'One more thing. You should change the order relating to ascetics. When we were returning after meeting Aayanar and his daughter, I saw a bikshu at a street corner. He quickly hid himself.'

'What is the order, prabhu?'

'The royal viharam must be placed under surveillance. We must find out about the bikshu who has just arrived.'

'I will arrange for this.'

Then, Commander Kalipahayar called the emissaries one by one and briefed the chakravarthy on which kottam each was heading to. Everyone took leave of the chakravarthy individually, leapt on their horse, and rode away swiftly.

8

Bhuvana Mahadevi

Mamallar, as instructed by his father, crossed the nila muttram, alighted from his horse and approached the inner entrance of the palace. The men in waiting took his horse away.

Then, Mamallar entered the beautiful palace and walked so fast that the torch-bearers had difficulty keeping pace with him. Those who were new to the palace would find it impossible to find their way around its labyrinthine paths. Narasimhar took several turns along those paths and reached the anthapuram. As soon as he reached the sculpted entrance, he heard a voice from within, 'My child! Have you come?'

The next moment, the chakravarthini of the Pallava kingdom, Bhuvana Mahadevi, reached the entrance of the anthapuram. The citizens of the Pallava kingdom called her the 'Chakravarthini of the Three Realms', because of her statuesque appearance and mature beauty.

The kumara chakravarthy called out 'Amma!' as he embraced her.

She began speaking, 'My child, today—' but Mamallar interrupted, saying, 'Amma! I beg of you. Please grant me a wish.'

Bhuvana Mahadevi smiled slightly.

'I will if you accede to mine,' she said affectionately.

When Mamallar responded saying, 'It is natural for a child to ask for a wish from his mother. But a mother never seeks a boon from her son,' Bhuvana Mahadevi stopped smiling. Both of them went in.

Narasimhar removed his turban and ornaments and washed his hands and legs. Both of them entered the prayer hall in the anthapuram. A beautifully decorated idol of Lord Nataraja stood in the middle of the prayer hall. Paintings on the wall behind depicted the myriad forms of Shiva and poses of the prankish Balagopal. As the prayer ceremony was already over, mother and son worshipped the deity and then entered the dining hall.

As soon as they sat down to eat, Bhuvana Mahadevi said, 'My child, apparently there is some important news. The gates of the fort have been closed. There is a lot of commotion in the palace. Only I don't know anything. Why don't you tell me? Do you also believe that women are inferior and need not be informed of anything?'

Mamallar glanced at the people serving food and said, 'Amma, once we finish eating, let's go to the upper storey, where I will tell you everything. But I have a request to make right away. Henceforth, do not wait for me to have dinner. Please stop this practice today.'

The empress looked at her son affectionately and smiled. But she did not respond.

In the Kanchi palace, lunch was an elaborate affair, in accordance with royal traditions. Senior government officials, premieres of foreign countries, Saivite and Vaishnavite saints, famous artistes, Tamil scholars and exponents of Utthara Bharata languages were invited. Hence, it was impossible to converse freely then. Also, the chakravarthy and the kumara chakravarthy were occupied with matters of the state during lunchtime. This is why the chakravarthy had arranged for mother and son to meet during dinner. Then, the three of them met in the upper storey of the palace.

Today, after dinner, Bhuvana Mahadevi and Mamallar went to the moonlit hall at the upper storey of the palace and sat on a platform embedded with crystals. Kanchi, which was drenched in milky white moonlight, was uncharacteristically calm.

Narasimha Varmar's heart reached out to the eastern gate of the fortress. Now, a palanquin must be exiting the eastern gate. Aayanar and his daughter would be seated in that palanquin.

Ah! They were in grave danger today. Who was the youth who had flung the spear at the mad elephant?

Bhuvana Mahadevi waited for her son to initiate the conversation. Realizing that he was immersed in deep thought, she said, 'My child.'

Immediately, Mamallar looked up with a start like someone who was awoken from a deep reverie.

'Amma, I will now seek the boon I desire from you. Henceforth, please do not call me "child". Am I still a baby? Even after defeating the reputed wrestlers of the Pallava kingdom and winning the title "Mamallar", you call me a child. Appa still treats me like a baby who is not yet out of his cradle. I am caught between the two of you . . .'

Hearing someone say, 'What can be done? For parents, their son is always a child,' the duo looked around. When they realized that Mahendra chakravarthy was standing behind them, they stood up deferentially.

Once Mahendra Varmar sat on the crystal platform, they followed suit. He then asked, 'Devi! Did our child say something?'

'He has not said anything yet. He is finding fault with both of us!'

'What can I do but find fault, appa? Even after receiving the news of enemies entering the Pallava kingdom, should we sit with our arms crossed? It seems as though Kali Yuga will end by the time Commander Kalipahayar mobilizes an army. Shouldn't our army have proceeded to war by now?' fumed Mamallar.

'Have our foes entered the Pallava kingdom? What is this?' asked Bhuvana Mahadevi, in a surprised and disbelieving tone.

'Yes, devi, they have not merely entered. They have suddenly entered with a massive army . . .'

'My lord, why have you prohibited me from talking at the ministers' council? When people were expressing their views, I had to restrain my anguish with great effort.'

The chakravarthy ignored Mamallar and addressed his chief consort. 'Devi, Narasimhan is still a child. He has not realized the gravity of the impending war. Both of you listen. The king of Vatapi, Pulikesi, has crossed River Tungabhadra and entered our kingdom with a huge army. I heard that his army consists of lakhs of foot soldiers, thousands of elephants, hundreds of carts harnessed by powerful bulls and sixteen thousand horsemen. Our spies have somehow been cheated. Pulikesi's demonic army has effortlessly defeated our border forces and is rapidly advancing. We do not have the forces to stop Pulikesi's army. Our forces stationed at various locations are retreating. The Pallava kingdom is in grave danger. But by the grace of Lord Pinakapani who burned down Tripura with his third eye, we will ultimately win. There is no doubt about that!'

Narasimhar, who was patiently listening till his father stopped talking, said, 'Appa, are the Pallava forces retreating? What a shame! Please allow me to proceed to the battlefield with the available forces!'

'Be patient, Narasimha. The time will come for you to lead the Pallava forces. Till then, please obey my orders. Tonight, there is an important task to complete. Do you want to come with me?'

'Do you have to ask? I will come, appa.'

'Devi, from today, I am not going to treat Narasimhan like a child but as a peer. I will grant him the right to participate in the ministers' council. You too don't address him as a child,' said the chakravarthy.

After asking Bhuvana Mahadevi to go to bed, father and son left the palace.

9

Freedom

As Paranjyothi climbed the rope and neared the roof, two vice-like hands lifted him by his arms. The next moment, he found himself standing on the roof. Naganandi was gesturing to him to remain silent. Another young bikshu was standing behind him. As soon as Naganandi signalled to him, the young bikshu coiled the rope, placed it in an ochre cloth and bundled it.

As Paranjyothi stood on the roof and surveyed the area surrounding the prison, he observed the top storeys of the mansions in Kanchi glistening in the moonlight. Meanwhile, the senior bikshu replaced the tiles to cover the hole in the prison roof and gestured to Paranjyothi to follow him. Paranjyothi and the young bikshu followed him over the roofs of houses and buildings carefully, without making any noise. If any noise was heard on the street, Naganandi gestured to them to sit down. When the noise receded, they resumed walking.

After the trio walked over the roofs of seven to eight houses, they reached a house located at the corner of a street with a lush growth of panneer trees in front of it. Bunches of flowers amidst the thick green leaves glowed like silver in the moonlight. Along with the gentle breeze wafted the fragrance of these flowers in all directions.

The bikshu carefully observed the street and then climbed down the trunk of a panneer tree. Paranjyothi and the young bikshu followed suit. They walked for a short distance and reached a beautiful building that resembled a temple. That building was the largest viharam in Kanchi. It was known as the 'royal viharam'. The sacred tooth of Lord Buddha, the epitome of kindness, was ensconced in the sanctum.

Though the Pallava kings had followed different religions at various points of time, they used to treat all religions equally and award grants to religious establishments. The royal viharam also received such a grant.

In those days, certain wealthy people in Kanchi practised Buddhism. One such person was a trader whose only son contracted a disease. He had vowed to renovate the royal viharam should his son recover. Since his son was cured, he renovated the royal viharam, incurring great expenditure. The viharam, coated with shell plaster and glistening in the moonlight, was an embodiment of beauty. Paranjyothi, seeing the viharam, exclaimed, 'Ah! What a beautiful temple!'

The bikshu closed Paranjyothi's mouth with a start. At that point of time, they had moved away from the shade of the panneer trees and were standing in the open area in front of the viharam.

At the same time, two white horses emerged from the dark shadows of the row of buildings opposite the royal viharam. Two warriors were seated on the horses. One was a middle-aged man and the other was a youth. Both were sporting large turbans. As both the warriors approached the viharam, the elder warrior said in greeting, 'Buddham saranam gacchami.'

The young bikshu responded, 'Dharmam saranam gacchami.'

'Adigal, aren't you aware that no one is supposed to be outdoors beyond midnight?' asked the elder warrior.

'I know, but I did not know that the order also applies to bikshus,' said the bikshu.

'Where are you going in the dead of the night?'

'This lad is my disciple. He is new to Kanchi and lost his way. I searched for him and fetched him.'

'Where does this youth come from?'

'From Sengattankudi in the Chola kingdom.'

'You two must have arrived today.'

'Yes, aiyya.'

'What is your name?'

'Naganandi.'

'Swami, don't venture out in the night henceforth. Inform your disciples too.'

After the warriors patted their horses and rode away, the trio entered the viharam. As soon as they entered, the outer gates of the royal viharam were shut.

Paranjyothi was stunned at the sight of the sanctum decorated with rows of lamps. The fragrance of incense that emerged from the sanctum made him slightly dizzy.

The bikshu placed his hand on Paranjyothi's head and said, 'Son! You were in grave danger. You escaped by the grace of Lord Buddha.'

Paranjyothi looked at him and asked, 'Adigal, what danger are you referring to?'

'Great danger befell you at the very entrance of this viharam. Did you recognize the people on the horses?'

'How would I know, aiyya? I am new to Kanchi.'

The bikshu whispered in Paranjyothi's ears, 'It was Chakravarthy Mahendra Varmar and his son, Mamalla Narasimha Varmar.'

Paranjyothi was startled. He asked, with amazement, 'Is that true?'

'Yes. Both of them were riding across the city incognito. Mahendra Varmar is unrivalled in assuming disguises.'

Paranjyothi was shocked. He then asked, 'What danger could they pose to me?'

The bikshu smiled mockingly and said, 'What danger could they pose to you! Had they known you were the one who hurled the spear at the elephant, it would have been impossible for you to escape. What do you know of the kumara chakravarthy? He cannot tolerate anyone who is stronger or braver than him. If he meets such a person, he will defeat that person in a wrestling match or send him to Yama Loka.'

'I will not shy away from a duel, even if it is with the crown prince,' said Paranjyothi.

'I know, my boy. It is because you're such a fearless warrior that you're likely to face greater danger. They will falsely allege that the temple elephant ran amok because you hurled the spear at it, and they will punish you.'

Paranjyothi's heart missed a beat. He recollected the conversation he had heard as he lay on the stone platform by the road. Paranjyothi, who had thus far not trusted Naganandi, started believing his words.

'Is such injustice possible?' he asked

'Paranjyothi, this is the hereditary trait of the Kanchi Pallavas. One hundred and fifty years ago, a youth like you named Mayurasanman came to Kanchi to educate himself. The Pallava kumara chakravarthy, envious of Mayurasanman's valour, framed false charges against him and imprisoned him.'

'Then?'

'Mayurasanman escaped from prison and established an independent kingdom on the banks of the Krishna River. He then took revenge on the Pallavas. By Lord Buddha's grace, like Mayurasanman, you too were saved from grave danger.'

Paranjyothi interrupted and said, 'Your holiness, forget the other dangers. Now I am in danger of losing my life because of hunger.'

Naganandi took Paranjyothi to the kitchen and served him food. He then took Paranjyothi to a veranda and said, 'Paranjyothi, you lie down here. I will give you a muhurtham to sleep. Sleep well. You are not completely safe from the danger that befell you. We should leave the fort before dawn.'

Paranjyothi immediately lay on the floor of the veranda. Nitra Devi possessed him.

10

Blindfolded Magic

Paranjyothi closed his eyes as soon as he lay down. But he was unable to sleep soundly. He had terrible nightmares that marred his sleep.

He dreamt that five to six bikshus had surrounded him. One of them held an illuminated lamp close to Paranjyothi's face. It seemed as though someone said, 'Yes! What Naganandi said was true. His physiognomy indicates that he will become either a great warrior or a saint.'

He dreamt that an elephant which had run amok chased him. He quickly climbed a panneer tree. He hurled a branch with bunches of flowers at the elephant. Suddenly a few horse-borne warriors appeared and exclaimed, 'You sinner! Have you killed the temple elephant?' Then they hurled their spears at him.

He had another terrifying dream. Naganandi stood next to him and stared at him intently. Even as Naganandi was staring at Paranjyothi, his face transformed into a cobra which was dancing with its hood spread out. That snake was about to bite his face with its thin forked fangs.

Paranjyothi woke up screaming. Naganandi was indeed standing beside him and looking at him. He asked, 'My son, why are you screaming? Did you have a nightmare?'

Paranjyothi responded, 'No aiyya, it's nothing. When you suddenly touched me, I was taken aback.'

'Dawn is only one muhurtham away. Let's leave. We need to leave the fort before dawn.'

'Why aiyya?'

'It is Lord Buddha's order.'

'To whom?'

'To me. I have been ordered to save you from danger. Don't you trust me even now?' asked Naganandi in a gentle tone.

Paranjyothi kept quiet.

'That's all right, just listen to me for the next one muhurtham. I will carry out Lord Buddha's orders. I will lead you out of this fort. Then, do as you wish.'

Paranjyothi was unable to refuse this request made in a very kind tone. He said, 'If you say so, adigal.'

'Will you obey me for the next one muhurtham?'

'I will.'

'Even if I were to blindfold you and take you from this place?'

Paranjyothi was shocked for a moment and then said, 'As you please.'

Immediately Naganandi blindfolded Paranjyothi with a small piece of cloth.

'My child, please walk holding my hand. Do not remove the blindfold till I ask you to. Someday, you will realize the benefit of obeying me today.' So saying, Naganandi started walking, holding Paranjyothi's hand. Paranjyothi's heart was beating wildly. Nevertheless, he strengthened his resolve and followed the bikshu.

Initially, Paranjyothi thought that they were crossing the viharam's entrance. Then, he felt they were walking by the road. From the fragrance of the panneer flowers, he conjectured that they could be passing the place where they had climbed down the panneer tree from the upper store of a house the previous night.

When they had walked for some time, they changed the direction in which they were walking. He could again smell the panneer flowers. He thought, 'Are we retracing our steps? This wicked bikshu could be doing this so that I don't find the way.'

It seemed as though they had again entered a building. Smelling the smoke from the incense, Paranjyothi decided that it was the royal viharam. Then Paranjyothi felt they were going through a dark serpentine cave. As his eyes were blindfolded, he felt as though they had been walking for an indefinite period of time.

'Aiyya, how long are you going to continue with this blindfolded game?' Paranjyothi asked.

'Son, we have almost reached. Please be patient for some time,' said the bikshu. Suddenly, Paranjyothi realized that he had stepped from darkness to light.

'Paranjyothi, we have reached our destination. The blindfolded ordeal is over.' So saying, he removed the blindfold.

Paranjyothi thought that they had reached the heavens by the grace of Lord Buddha. A beautiful sight met his eyes. In the backdrop, the ramparts of the fort rose perpendicularly. The silver rays of the setting moon had transformed the waters of the moat into molten silver. Beyond the moat lay a dense forest. Rays of moonlight frolicked with the leaves.

A boat was sailing in the moat. The young bikshu who had assisted in rescuing Paranjyothi from the prison was in the boat, holding an oar.

Naganandi and Paranjyothi got into the boat, which the young bikshu started rowing.

'Why do we need a boat to cross this moat? Couldn't we easily swim across?' asked Paranjyothi.

'Yes, those who know how to swim may do so.'

'How does this moat enhance the security of this fort? Enemies could easily swim across.'

'Look there!' said the bikshu. At a distance was a crocodile with its terrible jaws open.

'Oh no!' exclaimed Paranjyothi

'Hundreds of such crocodiles reside in this moat. During peaceful times, they are in cages. During wartime, they are let loose. Last night, they must have opened the cages.'

'In that case, is it true that there is an impending war, aiyya?'

'Why do you think there is so much commotion then?' asked the bikshu.

Paranjyothi kept quiet. The boat reached the opposite bank of the moat.

11

Aayanar, the Sculptor

The branches of the tall trees in the forest seemed to touch the sky and were closely intertwined. Amidst the thick foliage was a beautifully sculpted house.

It was dawn, about a jaamam after sunrise. One could hear the sound of leaves rustling in the gentle spring breeze. Birds chirping at different octaves created a beautiful melody.

Large granite boulders lay scattered beneath the trees that surrounded the house. Young sculptors armed with chisels were working on the granite boulders, either individually or in groups of twos and threes. The *kal kal* sound made by the chisels mingled with the sounds of the leaves rustling and the birds chirping, and intoxicated the listeners.

Amidst this melodious environment, suddenly a *jal jal* sound came from the house. The young sculptors, hearing this sound, stopped their work in unison. Their faces glowed with happiness.

The reason for their happiness was the sound of the anklets of their teacher's daughter, Sivakami. For three days, Sivakami had been inexplicably morose. Today, the sound of the anklets indicated that she had overcome her sorrow and had started dancing again.

After listening to the mellifluous anklets for some time and communicating with each other through facial expressions, the sculptors resumed work.

Before entering Aayanar's sculpture studio, let us understand the reason for his residing in the middle of a forest. During Mahendra Chakravarthy's reign, a wondrous cultural renaissance was taking place in the Pallava kingdom that extended from the border of the Pandya kingdom in the south to the Krishna river in the north.

In the ancient land of Tamil Nadu, talented painters and sculptors were propagating their respective arts. The art of sculpting temples out of hills and statues out of rocks spread everywhere. At the same time, the Saivite and Vaishnavite faiths regained acceptance in Tamil Nadu. Saivite and Vaishnavite saints, under the pretext of pilgrimages, travelled across the state, propagating their faiths. This had kindled heated debates among the already established faiths in Tamizhagam, i.e., Buddhism and Jainism, and the currently re-emerging Saivism and Vaishnavism, in support of their respective philosophies.

Intense rivalry developed among the four sects in Tamil Nadu, and it had a perceptible impact on the arts. The followers of each faith tried to propagate the art form associated with their faith.

All of them erected their respective places of worship across the country. There was a lot of competition for rocks and hills too, with each faith claiming ownership over them. The desire to sculpt places of worship and statues was the underlying cause for such claims.

Similarly, there was a lot of demand for sculptors and artistes. The followers of all the four faiths flocked to reputed sculptors and artistes. One such sought-after sculptor was Aayanar.

Aayanar, who was born, raised and educated in Kanchi, had come to be known as a great sculptor at a very young age. As his fame spread, his work was constantly interrupted. Several people ranging from Mahendra chakravarthy to ordinary citizens visited his residence, viewed his works and praised him. Aayanar spent a lot of time attending to his guests.

Aayanar, who was born in a Saivite family, was naturally devoted to Saivism. Also, he was attracted to the antique sculptures of Lord Nataraja. So, his sculptures were mostly associated with Saivism. Bikshus and Jain monks tried relentlessly to convert Aayanar to their respective faiths. To avoid these troubles, Aayanar decided to leave Kanchi and settle down in a house built in the middle of an uninhabited forest.

There was another reason that prompted Aayanar to leave Kanchi. Not only was Aayanar a great sculptor, but he was also an exponent of Bharata Shastram. His only daughter, Sivakami, showed indications of attaining proficiency in Bharatanatyam at a very early age. An intense desire rose within Aayanar. He resolved to teach Sivakami Bharatanatyam and to create lifelike sculptures of his daughter in various Bharatanatyam postures. He realized that he would not achieve his goals unless he left the city and relocated to a remote place.

Aayanar communicated his desire to Mahendra chakravarthy, who, understanding the eccentricities of artistes, immediately consented. He also volunteered to make the necessary arrangements for Aayanar.

Aayanar chose a location that was one kadu from Kanchi; it was in a dense forest, away from the highway. He built a house there and moved in with his daughter, Sivakami, and his widowed sister.

Aayanar's objectives that motivated his relocation to the forest were fulfilled to some extent. Sivakami's proficiency in dancing increased day by day. Aayanar initially sketched pictures of Sivakami's various dance postures. He then sculpted lifelike stone statues.

Though Aayanar moved to a secluded location, the world did not completely forget him. Artistes and connoisseurs of the arts frequently sought him out at his forest residence. Key people amongst the visitors were the chakravarthy, Mahendra Varmar and the kumara chakravarthy, Mamallar. There was an important reason behind their visits.

Once when the chakravarthy and the kumara chakravarthy had visited the Kadal Mallai port, the hills and rocks that dotted the landscape attracted their attention. They decided to create beautiful sculptures out of these hills and rocks and transform Kadal Mallai into a dream world.

As this idea had occurred to the kumara chakravarthy, the chakravarthy renamed the place 'Mamallapuram' and initiated the sculpting works. Thousands of sculptors from across Tamil Nadu came to Mamallapuram and started working there. The chakravarthy and Mamallar frequented Aayanar's residence to discuss ideas related to Mamallapuram and to review the progress. When they visited Aayanar's residence, they used to admire his sculptures of the various Bharatanatyam postures and appreciate Sivakami's dancing as well.

When Sivakami grew to be a young lady and had attained unparalleled proficiency in dancing, the chakravarthy ordered that her Bharatanatyam arangetram be held at the Kanchi court. We saw how the arangetram was interrupted earlier in the narrative.

12

Divine Art

Aayanar's house, located in the middle of the forest, was a feast to the eyes. When one entered the house after crossing the veranda and the front entrance, one could see large halls with a huge muttram and mandapam in the centre. The mandapam was elevated from the muttram. Sculpted pillars were erected at the corners of the halls. It was not evident if the pillars were built to support the mandapam or for decorative purposes.

On the walls were colourful paintings of Lord Nataraja performing various dances, like Nadandhu, Tandavam, Kunjitham and Oorthavam. Also, the abhinayams of a beautiful young girl were portrayed. Large boulders, broken boulders and boulders which were partially sculpted lay in the muttram.

On one side of the mandapam, completed lifelike sculptures were arranged in a row. Sculptures depicting the one hundred and eight postures mentioned in the Bharata

Shastram were fashioned after the same girl who was seen in the paintings.

But right then, those who entered the hall could not have concentrated on the wonderful sculptures because of the goings-on in the mandapam. The sight of the young girl, whose had posed for the sculptures, dancing must have captivated them. From her anklets emanated the sound *galir galir*. Aayanar was sitting at some distance from her and watching her with rapt attention.

Suddenly, Aayanar said, 'Stop!' That very instant Sivakami stopped dancing and stood still, holding her pose. Aayanar picked up his chisel and gently sculpted the eyebrows of an almost complete statue. He looked at Sivakami and said, 'Stay still for some more time, my dear.' He then worked further on the eyebrows. Then he said, 'That's enough, my child. Come and sit here.'

Sivakami sat next to Aayanar. He wiped the sweat off her face using his angavastram and said, 'My dear Sivakami, had the great author of the Bharata Shastram been alive today, he would have had to learn the intricacies of abhinayam from you. How well you convey emotions through the look of an eye and a twitch of an eyebrow! You were born for the sake of Bharatanatyam.'

'Enough, appa! I do not like any of these things,' said Sivakami in a tired voice.

'What is it you don't like?' asked Aayanar in a surprised tone.

'I don't like being a woman,' said Sivakami.

'Sivakami, what is this? For three days you said you were unwell. Why do you sound so detached? Are you angry with me for some reason?' asked Aayanar gently.

'Why should I be angry with you, appa? I am angry with the sage who authored the Bharata Shastram. I don't know why I learnt this art.' So saying, Sivakami sighed.

'Ah! Why do you utter such words? Are you angry with Bharata muni? Though you have attained unprecedented proficiency in dancing, you have not understood its greatness. The art of dancing forms the basis of all other arts. That is why it is called the divine art and the "Veda of Dance", endowed by Lord Brahma to Bharata muni. The art of sculpture derived its inspiration from dance. It also forms the basis of music. Those who do not know the Bharata Shastram will not be able to realize the soul of music. My dear, even Rudrachariar accepted this the other day . . .'

'Who is Rudrachariar? The man sporting a long white beard seated next to the chakravarthy?'

'Yes, he is the one. He is Mahendra Chakravarthy's music teacher. He has written treatises on music. Now he is very old. Despite his age, he came to your arangetram leaning on his staff. He was stunned seeing you perform. After the assembly had dispersed, he confided in me, "God bless your daughter. It was she who made me realize a truth. I have written treatises on music, which is a big mistake. Without learning the Bharata Shastram, writing treatises on music was a blunder." If a great music teacher like Rudrachariar is saying this . . .'

'Appa, how does it matter who said what? I don't like anything. What is the use of dance, music, sculpture and painting?'

'Sivakami! Are you questioning the utility of the arts? My child, you answer me. What is the use of the trees and plants in full bloom during spring? What is the use of the moon emitting milky-white rays on a full moon night? What is the use of the peacock dancing and the cuckoo singing? The utility of the arts is similar to these natural occurrences. There is a joy even in learning the arts. Haven't you experienced it? Why are you talking like this today, my child?'

Sivakami had a forlorn look in her eyes and did not respond. Two teardrops glistened like pearls in her wide black eyes.

Seeing this, Aayanar was startled and became immersed in deep thought. Then he gently patted Sivakami on her head and said, 'My child, I realize . . . I continue to treat you like a child. You have come of age and are aware of the world around you. You have seen girls of your age getting married and running households. Had your mother been alive, she would have pestered me to get you married. But, I haven't forgotten that duty either. Sivakami, of the one hundred and eight postures mentioned in the Bharata Shastram, I have sculpted forty-eight. After I complete sculpting the remaining sixty postures, I will get you married to a suitable groom.'

As Aayanar spoke thus, Sivakami wiped away her tears, looked up at him, and said, 'Appa, how many times have I asked you not to talk of marriage? I don't want to get married. I will not leave you alone and go away. I am not so cruel.'

The truth was that Aayanar was not really desirous of getting Sivakami married. He had brought her up with affection and also had personally educated her and taught her the arts. He thought he would not be able to be separated from her even for a minute. However, the thought of needing to give Sivakami away in marriage kept pricking him. So, he broached the subject of marriage with Sivakami from time to time. Sivakami's response that she did not want to get married would make him very happy.

Even today, Sivakami's response comforted Aayanar. Despite this, he continued, 'How is that possible, Sivakami? How can I retain you in my house without getting you married? Will society accept this? I have to get you married to a suitable boy. But a war is imminent, because of which the kumara chakravarthy's marriage is also delayed.'

There was a perceptible change in Sivakami's face at that moment. Excitement along with haughtiness enhanced her beauty.

'What are you saying, appa? Who is getting married? The kumara chakravarthy?' she asked.

'Yes! The queen is keen to get Mamallar married within a year. But the chakravarthy has said that the marriage may be solemnized only after the war is over. So, it is said that the chakravarthini is extremely sad.'

Sivakami said, in a voice tinged with anger, 'Appa, anyone may get married or not get married. But I certainly will not get married.'

Aayanar again said, 'How is that possible, Sivakami? How can girls born in Saivite families remain single? I am answerable to society.'

'Appa, you don't worry. I will embrace Buddhism and become a bikshuni. Then, no one will question you,' said Sivakami.

She had barely uttered these words when a voice chanting 'Buddham saranam gacchami' was heard at the entrance.

When they turned in the direction of the voice, they saw Naganandi adigal and Paranjyothi behind him. Paranjyothi was looking inside the house in wonderment.

13

Eternal Vision

As soon as Aayanar heard the bikshu's voice, he quickly stood up. 'Please come in, adigal.' So saying, he hastened to the entrance. Sivakami quickly got up and stood holding a nearby pillar.

The bikshu entered the house, looked around and asked, 'Aayanar, have you sculpted new statues since my previous visit?'

'Yes, aiyya. I have sculpted the twelve hand gestures. Please look here. All these statues are new,' said Aayanar.

The bikshu looked intently at the statues indicated by Aayanar. He then looked at Sivakami and asked, 'Is the figure next to the pillar also a statue?' The smile that appeared then on the bikshu's face made him seem uglier.

Aayanar laughed and responded, 'No, aiyya, she is my daughter, Sivakami . . . My child, this is Naganandi adigal. Please pay your respects to him.'

Sivakami had been looking at the youth standing behind Naganandi from the corner of her eye. As soon as she heard Aayanar, she turned towards the bikshu and prostrated.

Paranjyothi, who had followed the bikshu into the house, gazed at the sculpted wonders silently. He had not seen such beautiful sculptures and paintings before.

Now and then, he glanced at Aayanar and Sivakami. He realized that they were the ones who had been seated in the palanquin and whom he had rescued from the mad elephant.

Aayanar, who was animatedly conversing with the bikshu, did not notice Paranjyothi. But Paranjyothi observed that Aayanar's daughter was looking at him from the corner of her eye from time to time. Sivakami was adorned in her dance costume and jewellery. Paranjyothi was dazzled by Sivakami's beauty.

Paranjyothi, who had grown up in a village, was a reticent person by nature. He had not mingled with women, barring his mother. He was unable to even look at Sivakami's face. When he realized that Sivakami was observing him, he did not look in her direction. He studied the statues in the hall opposite to where Sivakami was standing. It occurred to him that there was a mystery in the appearance and expression in those statues.

The answer to the mystery occurred like lightning to him. The statues in various poses were fashioned after the girl leaning against the wall. When he realized this, he developed the kind of devotion one feels for God towards Sivakami.

When Sivakami prostrated before the bikshu, he stared at her intently and then said, 'May all your wishes come true by Lord Buddha's grace. Weren't you saying a little while back that you wanted to become a bikshuni?'

It was obvious from Sivakami's expression that she found the bikshu's blessing repulsive. The fact that Aayanar did not like the bikshu's blessing either was evident from what he said. 'Adigal! My child was saying that in jest. Four days ago, Sivakami's arangetram was held in Kanchi. It's a pity you missed it.'

'I heard about the arangetram and what happened after. It seems you were in great danger and you escaped from a mad elephant,' said the bikshu.

'Yes, aiyya. We escaped by God's grace. Are you free today? Today you must have bikshai with us.'

'Ah! I am free. I was thinking of having bikshai from your house, if it is of no inconvenience . . .' said the bikshu.

Aayanar interjected saying, 'Inconvenience? I am fortunate to host you.'

The two men sat on two large boulders in the courtyard, facing each other.

'Sivakami, why don't you sit too? Don't you know that the adigal is passionate about the arts?' After saying this, Aayanar asked in a hushed tone, 'Adigal, did you come to know anything of the Ajantha paintings?' Aayanar's boundless enthusiasm was evident then.

Sivakami did not sit despite Aayanar asking her to. She continued to stand, holding the pillar. Though she was listening to their conversation, she was also observing Paranjyothi.

The bikshu did not respond to Aayanar's query. Instead, he said, 'Aayanar, I believe that your creations are superior to those of God's.'

Aayanar responded, saying, 'Swami . . .'

The bikshu interrupted. 'I am not flattering you, Aayanar. I am stating the truth. God's creation is destructible. The human body cannot live beyond a hundred years. Age and sorrow affect humans. But the statues you sculpt are immortal. These statues are not afflicted by age and sorrow. The souls of these stone statues will shine ad infinitum. Is there any doubt that your creation is superior to God's?'

Hearing this, Aayanar's face exuded an artiste's pride.

'Adigal, this compliment rightfully belongs to Sivakami. Had she not attained unparalleled mastery over dance, how could I have sculpted these statues? Ah, it's a pity you were not present at my child's arangetram. Rudrachariar was stunned. I regret the absence of two people, you and Navukkarasar Perumal.'

'Oh yes, Aayanar. Navukkarasar would have been ecstatic had he been present at Sivakami's arangetram. Especially when she performed abhinayams to the chakravarthy's *Matha Vilasam*. The scene in which the intoxicated bikshus and kabalikas squabbled must have been particularly interesting.'

Aayanar frowned slightly. 'Swami, Sivakami chose the piece to demonstrate the hasya rasa. It was not her intention to mock great souls like bikshus.'

Mahendra Varma Pallavar, who was proficient in several arts and a connoisseur, had authored a humorous play titled *Matha Vilasam*. In this play, the kabalikas, meaning cannibals, and bikshus, were subject to great mockery. Sivakami had chosen a scene from the play to perform abhinayams. The above conversation was regarding this enactment.

Then the bikshu said: 'True, this was an apt sequence to demonstrate the hasya rasa. The scene where the kabalikas try to grab the bikshus' tufts and end up falling after fondling the bikshus' tonsured heads is extremely humorous. But I heard that, before the laughter in the court subsided, the chakravarthy received news of impending war and left the court.'

'Yes. That caused slight sorrow. That is why Sivakami was listless for four days. After the arangetram, she wore her anklets and resumed dancing only today. Adigal, why do wars break out? Why do people have to kill each other?' said Aayanar.

'What is the point in posing this question to an impoverished bikshu like me? This question should be directed to emperors, kings, crown princes, vassals and army commanders. Lord Buddha incarnated in a world filled with violence and cruelty and spread the faith of love. He also established bikshu sangas for this purpose. These are times when bikshus are mocked in royal courts. What is the use of asking me why wars break out?'

Sivakami realized that her father had got himself trapped in the clutches of the wicked bikshu by broaching the subject of war. She said, 'Appa, it is true that Lord Buddha preached the religion of love and non-violence. But these days fake bikshus, who profess to be followers of Lord Buddha, cheat and mislead people. That's why wars erupt.'

Aayanar, wishing to avoid an argument, looked sympathetically at Sivakami and started saying, 'My child, Sivakami. Why don't you go in and join your aunt . . .'

Naganandi interjected saying, 'Aayanar, I concede defeat. Sivakami is very bright. There is truth in what she said.' A strange smile appeared on the bikshu's harsh face.

Aayanar then looked around with the intention of deflecting the conversation. His eyes fell on Paranjyothi, who stood in another part of the hall looking at the paintings and sculptures.

'Swami, who is that boy? Is he your disciple?' asked Aayanar.

14

Lotus Pond

When Paranjyothi realized that they were talking about him, he turned around and faced them. At the same time, the bikshu said, 'Not my disciple, Aayanar. He is going to become your disciple. Paranjyothi, come here.'

Paranjyothi approached them. That's when Aayanar said in a surprised tone, 'Who is this boy? He looks familiar.'

'Appa, don't you recognize him? He is the person who hurled the spear at the mad elephant the other day,' said Sivakami enthusiastically.

Paranjyothi looked at Sivakami gratefully for a moment.

Aayanar's expression conveyed surprise and gratitude.

'What? Is he that brave youth? How skilfully he wielded the spear. Even Mamallar was amazed! Where do you hail from? Where were you all these days? When did he meet you?' Aayanar shot questions one after the other. Usually, Aayanar seldom displayed much interest in matters other than the arts.

'When I was returning from the Siddhar mountains, I met this boy on the way . . .'

Even as the bikshu started talking, Aayanar forgot Paranjyothi. 'Ah! Adigal. Did you visit the Siddhar mountains? Were you witness to the miracles performed by the siddhars?' he asked.

'I saw them, Aayanar. I will narrate them later. When I was returning, this boy was sleeping by the roadside. A huge cobra was about to bite him. I broke my penance of non-violence, killed the snake and rescued him . . .'

'This is amusing. Your name is Naganandi. You rescued him from the nagam. He prevented the "nagam" from killing us. Ha ha ha!' Aayanar said and laughed. As the word nagam can mean either snake or elephant, the pun on it amused Aayanar.

The bikshu said, 'Several things became possible because I rescued him. He bears a message for you.'

'Message? From whom?'

'From Thirvengadu Namasivaya Vaidhyar. This boy is his nephew.'

Aayanar stood up and asked enthusiastically, 'Are you my dear friend's nephew? What is your name, my boy?' Even as Aayanar was talking, he embraced Paranjyothi. Then he asked, 'Where is the missive?'

Paranjyothi looked at Naganandi. He said, 'Aayanar, as the message was lost, this youth was reluctant to meet you. That's why I brought him here. It seems that his uncle had sent messages to you and Navukkarasar through him. He had kept those epistles in his bundle. He lost the bundle where he hurled the spear at the elephant that night.'

Aayanar then said, 'Oh yes! There was a bundle lying close to where the elephant was standing. I brought it with me.

But the next day, the chief security guard of the fort sent someone to collect it from me. That's all right. Isn't it enough if you tell me that you are my dear friend's nephew? Do you need a written message? . . . Sivakami, this is the brave youth who saved us from grave danger. Did you convey your gratitude to him?'

Sivakami looked at Paranjyothi and said, 'I am not going to thank him. Who asked him to come in the way of fate and hurl the spear? Why could he not have minded his own business?'

The three people were taken aback by Sivakami's harsh words.

Naganandi looked at Aayanar and asked, 'Is your daughter feeling unwell?'

'That's not the case, swami. She has been morose ever since her arangetram was interrupted. She thought that it was a bad omen. Sivakami, please tell your aunt that the adigal has come,' said Aayanar.

Sivakami replied, 'Yes, appa.' She then walked towards the backyard of the house.

As she was passing through the rear entrance of the hall, she heard the bikshu utter the following words in a mocking tone. 'You should take good care of your daughter, Aayanar. Don't you know that when young girls lose interest in living, it is because they have become the target of Kama Deva's flower arrows.'

Sivakami said to herself, 'This bikshu is wicked. His heart and words are filled with venom. Why did my father befriend him?'

As Sivakami entered the middle part of the house, multiple sounds like *kal kal* and *chata chata* were heard in unison. Green and multi-hued parrots called out, 'Akka, akka.' Mynas cooed,

'Kee . . . kee.' Sparrows flapped their wings, which resulted in the *chata chata* sound. Peacocks that were seated on the roof of the courtyard flew and landed majestically on the ground. A fawn quietly walked up to Sivakami and looked up at her.

All these birds and animals were reared in the middle part of the house for Sivakami's recreation and for Aayanar's use as models in his sculptures and paintings. Hearing the noise they made as she entered the inner courtyard, Sivakami scolded, 'Keep quiet. What a headache!'

Immediately, an uncommon calm prevailed. Sivakami looked around and said, 'Today, I will take Rathi, who will come without making noise, along. Come, Rathi.' As Sivakami walked ahead, the fawn alone followed her. The other birds, though silent, looked at Rathi enviously.

The kitchen was located in the rear part of the house. Steam and the fragrance of food emanated from there. Sivakami, standing in the veranda, called out, 'Athai . . .'

'What is it, my child?' asked an elderly woman who appeared at the entrance of the kitchen.

'Two guests have arrived. The bikshu with a cat-like face, who had come earlier, is here,' said Sivakami.

'Don't talk of elders in this manner, my dear. Where are you going along with Rathi?' asked the elderly woman.

'Appa and that bikshu are arguing about something. I will spend some time at the lotus pond till they finish.' Saying this, Sivakami walked to the backyard of the house.

Jasmine creepers, Arabian jasmine, oleander and frangipani grew in abundance in the house's backyard. Sivakami walked beyond these creepers into a dense forest area. As she walked into the forest, she asked Rathi to follow her.

'Rathi, apparently my father is sad because two people did not witness my arangetram. Why should one be sad because the bikshu was not present at my arangetram? The person for whose affection I toiled ceaselessly and learnt dancing was not present. The greatest connoisseur in the Pallava kingdom did not come. Seven years ago, when I was a child like you, the person who adamantly insisted on learning to dance with me, the person who held my chin and pleaded with me to teach him dancing, did not come. Rathi, you tell me. Aren't men the most wicked people on earth . . . ?'

Poor Rathi, without realizing the significance of what Sivakami was saying, was nibbling grass tips. After they had walked for about ten minutes in the forest, they reached a clearing. In that clearing, there was a beautiful pond. Lotuses and water lilies abounded in the pond.

Sivakami stood at the edge of the pool and spoke as she looked at her reflection, 'Look, Rathi. If he comes again, I will not speak to him. I will definitely tell him, "Enough of your friendship. Go away."' Sivakami performed abhinayams to what she said.

A few minutes after Sivakami reached the pond, a high-breed horse traversed the forest. The warrior seated on the horse quietly descended from the horse and walked towards the pond.

15

Rathi—the Go-Between

Sivakami heard the sound of the horse approaching and realized that the warrior seated on the horse had alighted and was walking towards her. She was subconsciously aware of the identity of the person. Nevertheless, she was eager to turn around and confirm if her intuition was correct. Sivakami suppressed her curiosity and stood motionless like a statue.

The crown prince, Mamalla Narasimhar, came and stood next to Sivakami on the steps that led to the pond, holding a spear. In the clear waters of the pond, Sivakami could see Narasimha Varmar's reflection next to hers. Even then, Sivakami did not look at him.

A slight smile appeared on Narasimhar's handsome face. He, too, didn't look at Sivakami directly, but at the reflection of her moon-like face in the pond. Sivakami looked away immediately and asked the fawn standing beside her, 'Rathi, who is he? Ask him why he has come here.'

Hearing this, Narasimhar stopped smiling. His eyebrows knotted. He too looked at Rathi and said, 'Rathi! Now that my devi has become the unparalleled queen of Bharatanatyam in the country, how can she remember her old friend? I won't be surprised even if she asks who I am, Rathi.'

Sivakami said in an angry voice, 'Rathi! Please pay my respects to the chakravarthy's son, who is surprised by nothing, and also tell him this. He is the son of a chakravarthy. Kings of several countries pay their respects to him. How is it possible for him to be friends with this humble sculptor's daughter? I have realized that it is my stupidity to desire the unattainable fruit, Rathi.'

Mamallar said in a mocking voice, 'Rathi, remind your mistress about this. The Bharata Shastram exponent, Sivakami Devi, is not standing in a dance hall. She is not performing abhinayams. Please ask her to keep her dance, hand and face gestures aside and talk to me naturally.'

Sivakami's eyes reddened with anger.

'Yes, Rathi, I am a mere dancer. Compared to the son of the Kanchi chakravarthy, who is sculptor Aayanar's daughter? Several princesses at the anthapuram are keen to win his grace. How will he remember this poor girl who performs on stage?' As Sivakami said this, her voice faltered and her eyes filled with tears.

As Narasimha Varmar was soft-hearted, he asked in an affectionate tone, 'Sivakami, why do you speak like this? When I get to rule the Pallava empire, I will dedicate the kingdom to your beautiful anklet-adorned feet. Don't you know my feelings?'

Even after hearing this, Sivakami did not relent. She again looked at the fawn and said, 'Rathi, I have heard of the treacherous nature of men in stories and epics. But none of them come close to the Kanchi kumara chakravarthy.'

It was evident from the knotting of his eyebrows that Narasimhar was now truly angry.

'Sivakami! Why have you changed like this today? I came looking for you with so much affection and also thought of discussing several things. It seems as though you don't like my being here. I will leave now.' So saying, he took a step away.

Then Sivakami said in a choked voice, 'Rathi! If he wants to leave, he may do so. But ask him not to blame me.'

Narasimhar stood without moving further and said, 'What mistake have I committed? It would be good if you get angry after telling me where I have erred.'

Sivakami looked at him majestically, like a tigress, and said, 'You praised my dancing to no end and flattered me so much. After all that, why did you not come for my arangetram?' Sparks of anger darted from her eyes.

Narasimhar laughed heartily and said, 'Why didn't you ask this earlier? Who told you that I did not come to the arangetram? I sat with my mothers in the upper storey and watched. I was explaining the intricacies of Bharata Shastram to them. I was concerned that you might get distracted if I was in the court. Was this the reason for your outburst?'

Hearing this, Sivakami's face blossomed with a happiness not seen before. She looked at Narasimhar eagerly and asked, 'Why did you not tell me this earlier?'

'Where did you let me talk? I have to tell you much more. Come, let's sit on your throne and speak.' Narasimhar held Sivakami's hand and was about to lead her to the wooden plank under a tree, but Sivakami pulled her hand away and reached the bench with the agility of a deer.

Both of them sat on the wooden plank and Rathi looked at them. Realizing that her services as an emissary were no longer required, she started grazing on the lush grass at the banks of the pond.

16

Disrupted Wedding

Even after sitting on the wooden plank, Sivakami turned her face away. Seeing this, Narasimhar said, 'Why are you still angry, Sivakami? If you are still so obstinate, then I am bound to think that you don't love me.'

Sivakami immediately turned around, looked at Narasimhar, and said, 'As if you love me. If you did, why were you not reminded of me in the last three days?'

'I too was keen to meet you for the last few days. But there were important matters of state. Do you know why your arangetram ended abruptly the other day? The Pallava kingdom is about to face a war of a magnitude it has not witnessed for several years . . .'

Sivakami interrupted. 'I too have heard of it. So you have been worrying about the impending war.'

'Worrying? Never! Sivakami, war does not worry the Pallavas; it enthuses them. Since the times of my grandfather, King Simha Vishnu, there has been no war in the Pallava kingdom. The spears and swords held by the Pallava soldiers have rusted. Now, they need to be put to use. I am not scared of the thousands of spears and swords wielded in the battlefield. But I am scared of the spears and swords that fly from your black eyes.'

Sivakami, unable to suppress her smile, murmured, 'All men are the same. They hide the truth with their smooth talk.' These words did not escape Narasimhar's ears.

'You are levelling one charge after another. Which truth did I attempt to hide?' asked Mamallar.

'Did I say that you were scared of war? Don't I know that the grandson of King Simha Vishnu and the son of Chakravarthy Mahendra Varmar is a great warrior? Should a war break out, the wedding will be interrupted. I said that you were probably worried about this.'

As Sivakami spoke, shyness and anger battled on her face. Narasimhar asked in a surprised tone, 'Sivakami, what are you saying? Whose wedding has been interrupted?'

'Oh! It seems that you don't know anything. Shall I tell you? The son of Chakravarthy Mahendra Varma Pallavar of Kanchi is renowned all over the country. It seems arrangements were made to send emissaries to Madurai, Vanchi and kingdoms in Utthara Bharata to find him a bride. As a wicked king is about to invade the Pallava kingdom, the wedding has been postponed. Don't you know all this?' asked Sivakami.

Narasimhar laughed aloud and said, 'Is this why you troubled me so much? I was scared that Aayanar had arranged your wedding. I hope that is not the case.'

Sivakami's eyes glinted with mischief as she asked, 'Why not? My father often talks about my marriage. It seems that he is going to get me married to an accomplished sculptor disciple of his.'

When Narasimhar said, 'I am very happy. Did your father truly say that? I must immediately meet him and thank him,' Sivakami was shocked.

She continued in a mocking tone, 'But I did not consent. I told him that I do not want to get married. I am going to become a bikshuni.'

Narasimhar shot a volley of questions: 'What? Are you going to become a bikshuni? Is Aayanar's daughter talking thus? What harm did Lord Shiva and Tirumal cause you? Haven't you heard the nectar-like Saivite hymns composed by Thirunavukkarasar? Haven't you performed abhinayams to the divine verse "With lowered head and reddened lips . . ."? After all this, how did the thought of becoming a bikshuni occur to you?'

'I do not bear any grudge against Lord Shiva and Tirumal. I dislike marriage. I am going to become a bikshuni and travel across the country,' said Sivakami with her head lowered.

'Sivakami! Such a thought ought not to have occurred to you. How can you disobey a genius like your father? As per his wishes, you should marry his most accomplished disciple,' said Narasimhar in a harsh tone.

'Why are you so eager to see me married to some nincompoop? Did I prevent you from getting married to some princess?' said Sivakami. Tears glistened in her eyes.

'Careful, Sivakami! Whom are you calling a nincompoop? Don't you know who is the most accomplished of your father's disciples? Hasn't he said several times that no one is as proficient in sculpting as the kumara chakravarthy?

If you were to be married to Aayanar's most accomplished disciple, it has to be me. Shouldn't I thank your father for this?' When Narasimhar uttered these words, mischief and joy lit up his face.

Sivakami immediately stood up and said, 'My lord, why are you unnecessarily misleading this young girl . . .' Unable to speak further, she started crying.

Narasimhar held her hands, made her sit next to him on the plank, and said, 'Sivakami, haven't you still understood me? When I see you shed tears like this . . .' Sivakami interrupted him sobbing, 'My lord! These are tears of joy, not sorrow.'

17

Swearing by the Spear

As Narasimhar wiped Sivakami's tears away using the edge of his angavastram, he said, 'When I think about it, one thing surprises me.'

Sivakami looked up at Narasimhar just like Rathi had looked up at her some time earlier. She seemed to ask, with her quizzing eyes and knotted eyebrows, 'What is the surprising issue?'

Narasimhar looked at Sivakami as if he would devour her and said, 'I was referring to the changes you have undergone in the last three years. Do you remember, Sivakami? Those days, whenever the chakravarthy and I visited your house, you used to approach me without any bashfulness or reservation. You used to hold my hand and drag me away. When our fathers were talking, we were up to mischief. Sometimes, I used to ask you to teach me Bharatanatyam. You would teach me, but I was unable to perform well. Seeing this, you used to laugh aloud. I was mesmerized by your white, jasmine-like teeth. Occasionally, we used to play running and catching. You used to stand motionless amidst the statues Aayanar had sculpted. I used to pretend that I thought you were a statue and run ahead. Hearing you laugh, I would catch you. I then used to sing, "You have been trapped, Sivakami Devi!" Our fathers used to be happy, seeing us play thus. Now it seems that those times were a joyous dream.'

'My lord, you said that I have changed. In what way have I changed?' asked Sivakami.

'Good, you reminded me. When I was about sixteen years old, the chakravarthy had taken me along and travelled across the country. We travelled from the Siddhar mountains in the south to the Nagarjuna mountain in the north. We travelled up to the source of the River Kaveri in the west. It took us three years to complete the voyage and return . . .'

'Those three years seemed like three eons to me,' said Sivakami.

'When I saw you after three years, you were not the old Sivakami. It seemed as though Rambha or Urvashi from Indra's court was living in Aayanar's house. More than the change in our relationship, the change in your character and behavior surprised me. When you saw me, you neither came forward to welcome me enthusiastically nor did you chatter incessantly. You stood hiding behind a pillar. When I looked at you, you looked away. When I was not looking at you, you looked at me from the corner of your eye. Should our eyes meet accidentally, you lowered your head immediately. Your cheerful laughter had disappeared. Sometimes, your eyes were filled with tears. I observed you heave a sigh without reason. What surprised me the most was that I too started sighing without reason . . . ' When Narasimhar said this, Sivakami burst out laughing.

Narasimhar continued talking. 'I also felt a change within. I thought of you day and night. This thought gave me joy and sorrow at the same time. Even when I was engaged in the most important matters, I was unable to forget you. Under such circumstances, we met at this lotus pond. You fought with me for not having met you for the last three years. In the end, you asked me to promise you that I would not forget you. I was amused. Only I knew how I suffered without being able to forget you even for a moment. Despite this, I gave my word to satisfy you. After that, we are meeting by this pond only today. I was hoping you would be here, and when I came here, I found you just as I had wished. Our hearts beat in unison, Sivakami!' Saying this, Narasimhar stopped talking.

'You spoke so much. But you have not yet responded to my first question,' said Sivakami.

'What question was that? It would be good if you would remind me,' said Mamallar.

'Were emissaries about to be sent to Madurai and Vanchi to arrange your wedding?'

Narasimhar laughed slightly and said, 'That's true. Which mother would not like to see her son married? That's my mother's arrangement. But I was waiting for an opportune moment to share my feelings with the chakravarthy. The impending war has stalled it.'

'My lord, I am not at peace. I wish we were children, like we were three-and-a-half years ago.'

'No, Sivakami. Never! I will never consent to becoming children again. There are two reasons for this. First, after seeing Sivakami Devi, I cannot be in love with the child Sivakami. Second, would the chakravarthy, who objects to my going to the battlefield even now, have given his consent if I were a child?'

'My lord! Will you also go to the battlefront?' asked Sivakami in a worried tone.

'I will definitely go. I have been arguing about this with my father for the last three days. The Pallava kingdom, where no foreigner has entered for the last hundred years, is now being invaded by the Chalukyas. Should they not be routed and taught a lesson?'

'My lord, won't the Pallava army serve the purpose? Won't the army commanders do the job? Why do you have to go?'

'When the Pallava army is valiantly battling against the foes, what am I supposed to do? Am I supposed to feast in the palace and play dice with the ladies in the anthapuram? If I behave thus, will I be worthy of the love of Aayanar's daughter?'

Sivakami said, 'My lord, I am not the one to prevent you from going to the battlefield. Please go, vanquish our enemies and return. But . . .'

'But what?'

'I have a request, which you should not mock.'

'I will not, Sivakami. Tell me.'

'Just as Lord Subramaniar promised Valliammai, please swear by your spear that you will not forget me even in the battlefield.'

Narasimhar smiled slightly and said, 'Is that all? I will be unable to comply should you command me to forget you. I am willing to promise any number of times not to forget you. Look . . . !' As he held the spear aloft, he hesitated.

'My lord, why are you hesitating? Have you changed your mind so quickly?' asked Sivakami.

'No, Sivakami, never. This spear does not belong to me. How can I swear by a spear that belongs to someone else?'

'Is this spear not yours? Whose is it then?'

'It belongs to the valiant youth who rescued your father and you by flinging this spear at the mad elephant. I intend to meet that youth and return the spear to him.'

'After that incident, did you not meet that youth?' asked Sivakami.

'We have been searching for him all over the city for the last three days. We have been unable to find him.'

'What will you give me if I tell you where he is, my lord?' asked Sivakami.

'Do you know where he is? Tell me quickly, Sivakami! I have given myself to you. What else do I have to give you?'

'That youth is now in our house.'

Narasimhar got up with a start and asked, 'What are you saying, Sivakami? How did he come to your house?'

'Haven't I told you that a bikshu is insisting that my father and I travel to Utthara Bharata? It was that Naganandi adigal who brought that youth to our house.'

'Ah! What the chakravarthy said was true. Sivakami, listen to that!' said Narasimhar.

The sound of drums, conches and horse hooves was heard at a distance.

'Who, the chakravarthy?' asked Sivakami.

'Yes, the chakravarthy is coming. I will leave now and join him. Why don't you return home quickly?'

'I will go home through the shortcut. My lord! Will you come here before you go to the battlefield?'

'I will definitely come! I swear by the spears sparkling in your black eyes.' Narasimhar continued to look back at Sivakami as he hurriedly mounted his horse.

Sivakami gazed at him joyously. As soon as the horse disappeared into the forest, she quickly walked towards the house. The agility and enthusiasm that had been absent as she left her house were now evident in her stride. She forgot about Rathi. But seeing Sivakami leave, Rathi followed her with a sprightly gait.

18

Pearl Necklace

During the night when the news of the impending war broke out and the mad elephant caused chaos, chakravarthy Mahendra Pallavar was introduced to the reader as an unparalleled ruler amongst ancient Tamil kings, and as someone who sculpted his fame for eternity in (the) stone (sculptures).

Even the court poets of mere vassals used to compare their rulers with Brihaspathi for wisdom, Goddess Saraswati for learning, Manmadan for looks, Arjuna for bravery and Karna for charity. But in Mahendra Chakravarthy's case, such descriptions were not untrue.

Mahendra Varmar was a well-built personality. In his majestic face was evident the valour that came from an unbroken royal lineage of several centuries and the radiance that education and training in the arts endowed. The crown, crafted by the famed goldsmiths of Kanchi, earrings, armbands and veerakazhal adorned him. Multicoloured navaratna necklaces decorated his broad chest. Even in those days,

Kanchi was reputed for smooth silks of uncommon beauty and high quality. The weavers of Kanchi proudly stated that such silks appeared even more beautiful when Mahendra chakravarthy draped them.

Mahendra Varmar had attained scholarly proficiency in Tamil, Sanskrit and Prakrit. Scholars and connoisseurs from Taksashila in the north to Kanyakumari in the south flocked to Kanchi to demonstrate their expertise to the chakravarthy and win awards.

Many people felt that after Chandragupta Vikramaditya, who had ruled from Ujjaini in Utthara Bharata five hundred years ago and patronized Kalidasa and several other great poets, it was Mahendra chakravarthy who was a karpaga vruksha, wish-fullilling tree, to scholars and poets.

As the chakravarthy was passionate about sculpture and painting, he underwent training in these arts and attained a high degree of proficiency that surprised even the exponents of these arts.

Amazed at Mahendrar's uncommon creativity, expert sculptors bestowed the title of 'Vichitra Siddhar', meaning wonderful seer or visionary, on him. Similarly, painters conferred the chakravarthy with the epithet 'Chithrakara Puli', meaning tiger amongst painters. He authored a satirical Sanskrit play titled *Mathavilasa Prakasanam* and earned the title 'Matha Vilasar'—author of *Matha Vilasa*.

Mahendrar had studied music with the eminent musician Rudracharya, and had learnt to play a seven-stringed veena called 'parivadhini' with uncommon ease. Due to his expert handling of the sankeerna jathi tala, he was designated as 'Sankeerna Jathi Prasuranar'.

Mahendrar had followed Jainism when he was young and embraced Saivism later in life. So, he was tolerant towards all religions. The Saivites, the Vaishnavites, the Buddhists and the Jains in his kingdom were treated justly and fairly, which resulted in his being called 'Gunabarar', the virtuous one. As he donated money to build a Shiva temple in Thiruvathigai, the place came to be known as 'Gunabareshwaram'.

For about three hundred years preceding Mahendra Chakravarthy's reign, scholars, poets, Jain monks and bikshus from Utthara Bharata had migrated continuously to Dakshina Bharata, and had established educational institutions at Kanchi. So, during the time of this epic, Sanskrit and Prakrit had overshadowed Tamil. However, Saivite Nayanmars, such as Thirunavukkarasar, and Vaishnavite Alwars, like Poigai Alwar, were composing devotional hymns in Tamil and had begun restoring the prominence of the divine language. The reason for most of Mahendra Chakravarthy's titles being in Sanskrit and Prakrit will now be evident to the readers.

The King of Kings—Lord of the Earth—Chakravarthy of the Three Realms—Matha Vilasa—Vichitra Siddha—Sankeerna Jathi Prasurana—Chithrakara Puli—Gunabarar—Mahendra Varma Chakravarthy reached the entrance of Aayanar's house. On hearing the faraway trumpet sounds heralding the chakravarthy's arrival, Aayanar rushed to the entrance to welcome him and to extend courtesies.

As the chakravarthy alighted from his horse, he asked, 'Aayanar, was your return journey the other night comfortable? Is Sivakami doing well?'

Aayanar took a step forward, bowed and said, 'Ah! We reached safely. My child has not been feeling well for the last three days . . .'

Mahendra Pallavar interjected to ask in a concerned tone, 'Is that so? How is she feeling now?'

'Today, she is feeling better,' said Aayanar.

Everyone went inside the house. Aayanar had sculpted a beautiful stone throne to seat the chakravarthy whenever he visited them. As soon as Mahendrar sat on that throne, Aayanar gestured to Sivakami, who came forward and prostrated before the chakravarthy.

Aayanar then said, 'Perumane, as the arangetram was interrupted, Sivakami was listless. This is the reason for her not feeling well. Being a connoisseur of arts, please bless and encourage her.'

'Aayanar, it did not occur to me that Sivakami was dancing the other day. It seemed as though the very art of dancing had assumed a human form and performed,' said Mahendrar.

'I choreographed a piece set to Sankeerna jathi. She was unable to perform that item the other day,' said Aayanar in a dejected tone.

'Oh yes! I realized several wonders were to unfold. The sorrow I felt when I left the performance midway is indescribable. Had it not been an issue of the utmost importance, I would not have left,' said the chakravarthy.

'I too heard, prabhu! Is it true that foes are about to invade our kingdom? What audacity! How dare they do so!' exclaimed an enraged Aayanar.

'They will be punished for their audacity. For several years, enemy armies have not entered the Pallava kingdom, Aayanar. My father had sent me to Lanka to gain first-hand experience of war. But Narasimhan is fortunate to experience war right here. The king of Vatapi, Pulikesi, has mobilized a large army and is invading us. It will be necessary for us to gather a massive army and wage a bitter war. But mark my words. The anger I felt when Sivakami's arangetram was interrupted far exceeded my anger on hearing of the Chalukya invasion. They are bound to bear the punishment for this crime!' proclaimed Mahendrar.

Hearing this, Aayanar beamed with pride and shot an affectionate glance at Sivakami, who was standing nearby with her head lowered.

The chakravarthy further said, 'I had planned so much for the arangetram. It was not possible to execute my plans. I propose to extend the honour that ought to have been bestowed at the court. I hope you don't object . . .' So saying, the chakravarthy removed a beautiful two-strand pearl necklace from the bejewelled bag he held.

'Perumane, when you are bestowing the award, does the venue matter? Sivakami! You are very fortunate. Vichitra Siddha Maha prabhu, who understands best the intricacies of all the arts in the Bharata Kanda, is appreciative of your artistic talent and is about to honour you.' Speaking thus, Aayanar gestured to Sivakami, who stepped forward, humbly bowed to the chakravarthy and extended her hands.

As Mahendrar placed the pearl necklace in Sivakami's hands . . . Ah! Again a bad omen. The necklace slipped from her hands and fell on the floor.

Aayanar's face immediately fell. Even Mahendra Pallavar's firm resolve was slightly shaken; this was evident from the knotting of his eyebrows.

We cannot know if Sivakami's heart also trembled. But the very next moment, it was evident from the colour in her face that she certainly felt ecstatic.

The kumara chakravarthy had picked up the pearl necklace the very instant it fell down. He placed it in Sivakami's extended palms. Sivakami devotedly touched the pearl necklace to her eyes and wore it. It is but natural that the joy Sivakami felt on receiving the pearl necklace from the kumara chakravarthy was reflected on her face.

19

The Buddha Statue

Aayanar's face glowed when he observed the kumara chakravarthy handing the pearl necklace to Sivakami.

The chakravarthy, though seemingly unobservant, noticed this incident too. He addressed the great sculptor. 'Your daughter will be conferred several priceless awards like this pearl necklace in the future. She will enhance the fame and greatness of the Pallava kingdom. Whatever happens in future, Sivakami's dance training should not be interrupted for any reason. You should ensure she does not lose interest in dancing.'

Aayanar said, 'Pallavendra, when you and the kumara chakravarthy are so encouraging, why would Sivakami lose interest? Why should I worry?'

Mahendra Pallavar responded, 'That's not the case, Aayanar. It is likely that the crown prince and I will not be able to visit you for some time because of the war. There should be no interruption to both your artistic services on account of this. Didn't you tell me some time ago that Sivakami was desirous of becoming a bikshuni? That is a fitting decision. Sivakami is not like other girls, to get married at an appropriate age and spend her life indulging in transient pleasures. Only one woman in a lakh is endowed with such an artistic bent of mind. This should be nurtured and made to flourish. As far as married life is concerned, Sivakami should consider herself a bikshuni. She should devote herself to the divine art of dancing.'

One would never know what transpired in Mahendra Pallavar's mind when he uttered these words. But it was evident that his words aroused different emotions in the three listeners from their varying facial expressions.

Aayanar's words revealed his delight. 'My lord! You have echoed my sentiments. There are several women who get married and rear children. But there aren't many to learn this wonderful art and cause it to flourish.' As Aayanar was speaking, he turned to Sivakami and asked, 'Did you hear the chakravarthy's golden words, my child?'

At that moment, Sivakami's face resembled the emotionless face of a sculpture created by an amateur. Sivakami, who was capable of conveying a myriad of emotions through her expressions, through the flicker of her eyelids and the twist of her lips, did an excellent job of not giving away her feelings.

As Narasimhar was not trained in the art of abhinayam, his face reddened on hearing the chakravarthy's words. His lips twitched. Before others could observe it, he immediately stepped away, pretending to view the sculptures and paintings.

The chakravarthy also stood up from the sculpted throne on which he had been seated for so long and said, 'Respected sculptor, I have several important and urgent tasks. However, I forget those when I come here. I need to leave quickly after viewing your new sculptures.' As Mahendrar spoke, he walked towards the sculptures. Aayanar followed him.

As Mahendra Pallavar looked at the sculptures, he identified each pose, saying, 'This is Gajahastham, this is Arthashastra hastham.' He spoke as he walked and stopped before the statue Aayanar had completed last. He exclaimed appreciatively, 'Ah!' and looked intently at the statue for some time. He then said, 'Aayanar! You have no peers amongst the great sculptors of Thondai Mandalam,* but you too have not created such a lifelike sculpture before. The pathos arising from a long separation from a loved one is communicated beautifully through the facial expression and the arched posture. Even the eyes, eyelashes and eyebrows communicate with us. Aayanar, I presume you completed this statue after Sivakami's arangetram?'

'Yes, Perumane. I completed it this morning. Sivakami, mercifully, danced and performed abhinayams for me.'

Mahendrar shot a gentle glance at Sivakami and said, 'Respected sculptor, didn't the author of the Bharata Shastram state that there were seven abhinayams that could be performed using the eyebrows? Had he seen our Sivakami perform, he would have realized that seven hundred abhinayams could be performed using the eyebrows and would have written the Bharata Shastram accordingly.'

As the chakravarthy was talking casually and walking, his glance fell on a gigantic statue of Buddha. As he stood looking at the Buddha statue, he said, 'Ah! Buddha, who is the personification of kindness, tried to eliminate violence and

* Another name for the Pallava kingdom in Tamil.

war from earth. Wouldn't it be good if all the rulers on earth followed his advice? The only holy soul who followed his path was the Maurya Chakravarthy, Ashoka. After him, no king following the path of ahimsa has emerged in this nation.'

As Aayanar was silent, the chakravarthy said, 'Respected sculptor . . . Good! In all fairness, you must be punished as an enemy of the kingdom . . .' Aayanar's confusion was resolved by the words that followed.

'Yes, I intended to keep my visit short, but you made me stay for such a long time. Do you know how many tasks are unattended to? That's all right. I will forgive you this time.' Mahendrar walked towards the entrance smiling. The others followed him.

As soon as he crossed the entrance of the house, the chakravarthy turned to the sculptor and said, 'Aayanar, I do not know when I will return to your sacred temple of sculptures. This ancient Pallava dynasty may be destroyed at some point of time . . .'

'Perumane, never. Please don't say that!' shrieked Aayanar.

'Please pay heed, respected sculptor! Several empires have flourished and have come to naught in this world. Hastinapuram, Pataliputram and Ujjaini have disappeared without a trace. The Pallava dynasty may also come to an end one day. But your kingdom of art will never be destroyed. Your kingdom of art will flourish as long as the divine language of Tamil and Tamil Nadu exist!'

Aayanar then said in an emotional tone, 'My lord, several sculptors like me will evolve and pass away. Our names will be forgotten. But as long as sculpture and painting flourish in this country, you and the kumara chakravarthy will be immortal.'

How true were that great sculptor's words! The names of the sculptors who converted Mamallapuram into a dream world have disappeared. But haven't Mahendra Pallavar and Narasimha Pallavar earned an indelible place in history?

The chakravarthy and his son mounted the waiting horses. Mahendrar looked at Aayanar and said, 'See, I have forgotten an important matter. We need to discuss the works to be completed at Mamallapuram before I proceed northwards. Please reach the port by tomorrow noon.'

'Yes, your majesty. I will be there,' said Aayanar.

Aayanar and Sivakami stood at the entrance of the house watching the departing horses.

From the time Mahendra Pallavar reached Aayanar's house to the time he mounted the horse, he had conversed with Aayanar. Neither the crown prince nor Sivakami had uttered a word. But we cannot be sure that they did not communicate through their eyes whenever the opportunity arose. Finally, Narasimhar bid farewell to Sivakami through his eyes.

When Narasimhar had travelled some distance on the horse, he turned around. He observed Sivakami eagerly looking at him. Immediately, he held the spear aloft and smiled. The next moment, he turned his face away and patted his horse.

Sivakami understood the crown prince's gesture. Joy was evident in her eyes, eyelashes and eyebrows.

Sivakami watched till the horses disappeared into the forest, without blinking. Some more time elapsed before she thought of re-entering the house.

Delighted with Narasimhar gesturing to her by holding the spear aloft, Sivakami remembered the owner of the spear.

When Sivakami remembered Narasimhar questioning her about this through his eyes and she staring at him unable to respond, she felt like laughing. She intended to inquire of Aayanar, who had entered the house before her. As she entered the house, she saw Aayanar walking towards the Buddha statue, and the bikshu and the youth suddenly standing up from behind it. Sivakami felt an inexpressible shock.

20

Ajantha's Secrets

Why did the bikshu and Paranjyothi hide behind the statue?

What happened at Aayanar's house after a dejected Sivakami, accompanied by the fawn, headed to the lotus pond?

Aayanar had not liked the bikshu speaking of his dear daughter in a slightly inappropriate manner. So, he stopped talking to the bikshu and asked Paranjyothi, 'Thambi, please let me know if I may be of assistance to you.'

'I came to Kanchi to educate myself at Navukkarasar's monastery, aiyya. I would also like to learn the art of sculpting. My uncle asked me to meet you and to act as per your orders. He had written everything in detail in the missive,' said Paranjyothi.

'Why do you need written message, thambi? I am obliged to do everything for my dear friend. Navukkarasar Peruman is currently not in Kanchi; he has gone on a pilgrimage. So what? I myself will admit you to the monastery of that Shiva devotee. I need to take you to the chakravarthy.

The chakravarthy will feel extremely happy when he meets you who rescued us through your brave act . . .'

The bikshu interrupted saying, 'Please refrain from doing that, Aayanar, if you feel any affection for this youth . . .'

'Why, adigal?' asked a surprised Aayanar.

'Don't you know what the punishment is meted to those who escape from the Kanchi Chakravarthy's prison?'

'Why not? It's the death sentence. I do not know the purpose of your raising this question.'

'If he were to meet the chakravarthy, then he would be sentenced to death.'

'Shiva, Shiva! What are you saying? Was he in prison? When? Why?'

'He lost his way around the city the night he rescued you. The city guards suspected that he was a spy and imprisoned him.'

'Oh no! What happened afterwards?'

'That night he escaped from the prison.'

'What? How did he escape?'

'He came out through the roof . . .'

Aayanar looked at Paranjyothi in amazement and said, 'Ah! It seems that my friend's nephew cannot be taken lightly. He is extremely smart. That's all right, adigal! I myself will escort him to the chakravarthy and request him to pardon this boy. When the chakravarthy comes to know that he rescued us from grave danger, he will definitely pardon him!'

'True, he will be pardoned for your sake. But don't you know he may have to go to the battlefield as people are being enlisted to the army everywhere in the Pallava kingdom?'

Hearing this, Aayanar became immersed in deep thought. Observing this, the bikshu continued. 'He is the only child to his mother. If something happens to him on the war front, his mother will curse you. That's not all. Like Dharmasena's sister, another girl will have to spend her life without marrying.'

The comment pricked Aayanar. He thought that the bikshu was referring to his daughter. Was there truth in what he said? Had Sivakami been dejected for the last three days because she had fallen in love with this youth? If that was the case, then wasn't that good too? Sivakami had to get married. Wouldn't it be good if she could be married to his dear friend's nephew, who would also become his disciple? After thinking thus for some time, Aayanar looked at Paranjyothi intently.

The bikshu, realizing his intentions, said, 'No, Aayanar! What you're thinking cannot happen. His cousin in Thiruvengadu is waiting to marry him.'

Hearing this, Aayanar shot a glance at the bikshu that seemed to enquire, 'How did you read my thoughts?' He then asked Paranjyothi, 'Is that so, thambi? Are you going to marry my friend's daughter?'

Paranjyothi shyly responded, 'Yes, aiyya.'

The bikshu further said, 'It is not good to admit him at Navukkarasar's monastery now. The Kanchi fort is being fortified for the siege. Navukkarasar will not return to the monastery now. Apparently the chakravarthy has asked him to head to the Chola kingdom on a pilgrimage.'

'Adigal, you are so well informed, whereas I am totally ignorant,' said Aayanar, unable to contain his surprise.

'You are residing in the midst of this forest, so you are unaware. I roam around the country, so I'm aware,' said the bikshu.

Aayanar thought for some time and then asked, 'Thambi, there is so much confusion here. What do you want to do?'

'Aiyya, I told my folks in the village that I would return after completing my education. I do not want to return without learning some art. I would like to acquire some education and learn sculpture from you. Kindly accept me as your student,' said Paranjyothi.

Aayanar, who was ecstatic listening to Paranjyothi's humble words, said, 'Sure! You can stay here and learn sculpting from me.'

'What about acharya dakshina? You need to collect it in advance, Aayanar,' said the bikshu. Aayanar laughed, thinking that the words were uttered in jest.

'I am not joking. I am stating the truth. The guru dakshina which Paranjyothi needs to give you is the secret of the Ajantha paintings!' As soon as the bikshu uttered these words, uncontrollable eagerness was evident on Aayanar's face. At that moment, he seemed to have become a new person.

'Adigal, I asked you about this earlier, you did not say anything. But what is the connection between this boy and the secret of the Ajantha paintings? What can he do?' asked Aayanar.

'The secret has reached the Buddha sangramam at Nagarjuna mountain. We have to send someone there to fetch the secret. We cannot find anyone more suitable for this job than your new disciple.'

'Nagarjuna mountain? Isn't it on the banks of the Krishna River? Won't he face several dangers on the way?'

'He is a warrior who will overcome all dangers and return. Didn't you observe how he hurled the spear at the elephant?'

'Still, isn't it far away? How can he travel by foot?'

'He cannot. We need to procure a good horse for him. If a horse is available, he can accomplish the task and return in a month.'

Aayanar looked at Paranjyothi eagerly and asked, 'Thambi, can you do it? Will you go?'

A wide-eyed Paranjyothi responded, 'Sure, aiyya. I am ready to carry out your orders. But I do not understand where I need to go and the purpose of the visit.'

'True! He doesn't know the purpose of the visit. You tell him, swami.'

The bikshu looked at Paranjyothi and said, 'Listen, appane. In the north, beyond the Godavari River, lie the Ajantha mountains. Long ago, Buddha sangramams were carved out of the mountains. In these sangramams, wonderful paintings depicting Lord Buddha's life, his previous incarnations and greatness were sketched. These paintings are five hundred years old. Even today, the colours have not faded and the paintings seem like new. The descendants of the geniuses who sketched these paintings are still there. They are sketching new paintings adjacent to the ancient ones at the Ajantha caves. They know the secret of the additive that will prevent the paintings from fading even after a thousand years. Aayanar has been asking me to learn the secret and share it with him for a long time. I too have been trying. I know an artist at the Ajantha mountains who knows the secret method. I received news that he is residing at the Nagarjuna mountain Buddha sangramam these days. If you go there, you can learn the secret from him and return.'

As soon as the bikshu stopped talking, Aayanar said, 'Thambi, will you go there? If you bring back the secret, you will fulfil one of my life's goals. But, I will not compel you!'

Several confusing thoughts arose in Paranjyothi's mind. It is unnecessary to clarify that most of the confusion was joyful in nature. He was delighted at the idea of mounting a high-breed horse and travelling a long distance. He was also proud that he would be carrying out such an important task at the behest of the great sculptor, Aayanar. Such tasks suited his nature better than wielding a stylus to write.

'Aiyya, my uncle has asked me to act according to your wishes. If you order me to go, I will do so,' said Paranjyothi.

Naganandi adigal then said, 'There is no time to delay, Aayanar. It would be good if he could return before the Vatapi forces reach Kanchi. Can the horse be arranged?'

'That's not difficult. I will request the chakravarthy to provide a horse. Mahendra chakravarthy is as eager as I am to learn about the secret additive in the Ajantha paintings.'

'If that's the case, please also obtain the insignia for travel from the chakravarthy. As these are times of war, Paranjyothi may face hurdles on the way.'

'True. I will also obtain the insignia.'

'Please do not mention me in this conversation. You know the chakravarthy's views on bikshus.'

As the bikshu was saying this, the sound of trumpets and conches was heard at a distance.

'Adigal, the God whom we wanted to worship is approaching us. Here comes Mahendra chakravarthy,' said Aayanar enthusiastically.

A smile appeared on Naganandi adigal's stern face. He thoughtfully looked around. Then he spoke decisively. 'Aayanar, this is a good omen. The arrival of the chakravarthy at this time indicates that we will successfully achieve our objective. But Paranjyothi and I will hamper the proceedings. All our tasks would be halted midway if the chakravarthy were to see us. We will seek refuge in Lord Buddha during the chakravarthy's visit. What can one say about the foresight of the great soul, Nagarjuna bikshu, who established the practice of sculpting large-sized Buddha statues?'

Even as Aayanar hesitantly asked, 'What if he comes to know . . . ' the bikshu held Paranjyothi's hand, led him to the Buddha statue, and hid behind it.

As the sound of the horse hooves neared, Aayanar did not have time to think. He said, 'Careful, adigal,' and hastened to the entrance to welcome the chakravarthy.

So, when the bikshu and Paranjyothi emerged from behind the statue, Sivakami was taken by surprise, but not Aayanar.

In fact, Aayanar seemed to be more agitated than Sivakami was.

'Adigal! We were lucky. We escaped from great danger,' said Aayanar.

'Those who attain refuge in Lord Buddha will face no danger. Never mind. Just as in the story in which the horse is forgotten at an Ashwamedha Yagna, didn't you too forget to ask chakravarthy for a horse?' said the bikshu.

'I did not forget, adigal. The words uttered by the chakravarthy when he reached this place unnerved me. Then I was unable to bring myself to ask for a horse.'

'Yes, even I was taken aback when the chakravarthy mentioned that he was going to punish you for treachery.'

After the bikshu and Paranjyothi emerged from behind the Buddha statue, the three of them sat at the place where they had previously been sitting and continued with their conversation. As Sivakami also reached the place then, the bikshu looked at her and said, 'You have to tell Sivakami everything. She seems to think we are ghosts!'

21

The Painting at Siddhar Mountain

Of the fifteen emotive eye expressions, Sivakami shot a glance at the bikshu that conveyed doubt and disgust and asked Aayanar, 'Were these people here all this time?'

'Yes, my child.'

'Were they hiding behind the Buddha statue?'

'Yes! But you do not have to doubt this—'

Before Aayanar could explain further, Sivakami said, 'How useful it is to sculpt large-sized statues of Lord Buddha!'

'That's why I praised Nagarjuna bikshu who is the founder of the Mahayana philosophy,' said Naganandi.

For some time after the Buddhist religion was established, creating sculptures and paintings of Lord Buddha was prohibited. Two hundred years before the occurrence of this legend, a savant named Nagarjuna bikshu founded the Mahayana philosophy. Nagarjuna, who was the head of a reputed monastery at Nalanda in Utthara Bharata, travelled across the country, engaged in debates and propagated the Mahayana philosophy. He also set up monasteries named sangramam at several places. He established one such sangramam on the banks of the River Krishna on the Sri mountain. From then on, the Sri mountain came to be known as Nagarjuna mountain.

The Mahayana sect that Nagarjuna established allowed for temples to be built, and statues of Lord Buddha to be sculpted. Now that the Buddha statue had come to Naganandi's rescue, he was effusive in his praise of Nagarjuna bikshu.

Sivakami, not heeding what Naganandi said, asked, 'Appa! Why did they hide?'

'Amma, don't you know that our Naganandi adigal has vowed not to see royalty? Since this youth accompanied him . . .'

'Appa, the chakravarthy and Mamallar would have been so happy to see him. Didn't you notice? Wasn't Mamallar holding a spear? It belongs to this warrior . . .'

Naganandi again interrupted saying, 'What is so surprising about it, Sivakami? Doesn't the Pallava kingdom require weapons now? Aren't they accumulating all broken spears, swords and lances?'

Sivakami shot a fiery glance at him and said, 'Appa, it is possible that the kumara chakravarthy is retaining the spear with the express intention of returning it to the owner. Can anyone honour true warriors as much as Mamallar? You should immediately take him to the chakravarthy's court.'

Aayanar said hesitantly, 'Sure, amma, that's my intention too. As soon as Paranjyothi returns from his journey to the north, I will take him to the chakravarthy.'

Paranjyothi was silent all this time as he was ashamed of hiding behind the statue during the chakravarthy's visit and was naturally shy in Sivakami's presence. But Sivakami's words cut through the cords that seemed to bind his soul and tongue. He shot a grateful glance at Sivakami and told Aayanar, 'Aiyya, what your daughter says is true. I too think that the spear the kumara chakravarthy was holding belongs to me. It would be good if you could arrange for it to be returned to me. How can one travel a long distance unarmed?'

Then the bikshu said, 'What is the hurry for weapons? I will procure any number of spears and lances for you. The important task is not yet complete. Aayanar, you did not request for a horse and the insignia.'

'That's my responsibility. The chakravarthy has ordered me to come to Mamallapuram tomorrow. I will secure his approval for a horse and insignia there. Please attend to the other travel arrangements,' said Aayanar.

Sivakami asked, 'Appa, is this annan going to travel a long distance? To which place? Why?'

'I am sending him, my child. He is going for a very important matter, something I have been dreaming of day and night for the last nine years. Sivakami! My dream is about to be fulfilled through the assistance of this virtuous bikshu.' When Aayanar uttered these words, his face exuded uncontrollable eagerness, like before.

'What did you dream of? How is it going to be fulfilled? I don't understand anything,' said Sivakami.

'Haven't I told you of the wonderful colour paintings in the caves of the Ajantha mountains several times? I am sending this boy, my dear friend's nephew, to ascertain the secret of the additive that has preserved those paintings without the colours fading even after five hundred years.'

'How can a painting not fade even after five hundred years? I do not believe this, appa,' said Sivakami, shooting a look of disbelief at the bikshu.

'It is hard to believe. I was skeptical when I heard of this first. I too thought, "How can a painting not fade for over five hundred years?" Only when I viewed the paintings with my own eyes did I believe it,' remarked Aayanar.

When Aayanar said this, Sivakami and the bikshu conveyed their amazement in unison.

'Did you see the paintings? When?' asked Sivakami.

'You did not tell me this all these years. Have you been to Ajantha?' asked the bikshu.

'No, I have not been to Ajantha. But I saw it in the Siddhar mountains. Adigal, you too mentioned that you had been to the Siddhar mountains. What wonders did you see there?' asked Aayanar. The bikshu's face glowed.

'Ah! I know . . . I saw paintings of the Jain tirtankarars sketched in indelible ink. I saw paintings of two divine nymphs strike two rare poses mentioned in the Bharata Shastram at the entrance of the caves. I was wondering which great artist painted those pictures . . .'

'Did you recognize the painter, swami?'

'Now I do. Who else but the great Aayanar could sketch such lifelike paintings in Dakshina Bharata?'

'Yes, adigal, it was I who sketched those paintings. Did you notice any peculiarity?'

'The top half of the paintings of the nymphs glowed as though they were new. Below their waists, the paintings were faded.'

'Ah! The paintings would have faded in nine years' time,' said Aayanar. Then Aayanar hesitantly related the story of the Siddhar mountain paintings.

Twelve years earlier, when Mahendra chakravarthy was practicing Jainism, he took Aayanar along on a trip around the Chola kingdom. After enjoying the hospitality of the Chola king at Uraiyur, they proceeded to a famous school established by the Jain monks at Siddhar mountains. The chakravarthy and Aayanar were amazed at the colour paintings on the walls of the caves.

The monk who had sketched the paintings was residing at that mountain school. The chakravarthy and Aayanar did not believe the monk when he mentioned that the paintings would not fade even after a thousand years. They did not believe the ascetic even after he told them about the Ajantha paintings. Then the Jain monk threw a challenge. He asked Aayanar to sketch the outline of two nymphs at the entrance. He then asked Aayanar to paint the top half of the figures with the paints the monk had prepared, and to paint the bottom half with Aayanar's own paints. The paintings were to be reviewed after three years. If what the monk said was true, then Aayanar should embrace Jainism. The monk undertook to divulge the secret additive used in the paints once Aayanar embraced Jainism.

Agreeing to the condition, Aayanar painted the pictures of the nymphs using both the paints. When Aayanar returned after three years to view the paintings, he saw that the top half appeared the way it had when it had just been painted; the bottom half had greatly faded. Aayanar was surprised by this and prepared to embrace Jainism, as per the terms of the challenge, and learn the secret of the additive. But the Jain artist who had challenged him was not there. He, like several other enraged Jain monks, had left the Pallava kingdom after the chakravarthy had embraced Saivism. But Aayanar's keenness to learn about these indelible paints had intensified.

When Aayanar completed relating the above story, the bikshu said, 'Aayanar, don't worry. The time has come for your desire to be fulfilled. Your goal will be achieved within a short time of your arranging a horse and insignia for Paranjyothi.'

Paranjyothi enthusiastically said, 'Yes aiyya. It will be my fortune if your goal is achieved through me. I will not retreat in the face of danger and will return only after completing the task successfully.'

Contradictory thoughts occurred to Sivakami. She was aware of Aayanar's eagerness to unravel the secret of the additive, and the happiness he would experience should his goal be achieved. But she was afraid that there may be some treachery behind the assignment which was initiated at the instigation of the bikshu. So, she decided to meet Paranjyothi alone and warn him.

22

Shatrugnan

Mahendra Pallavar, after leaving Aayanar's house, rode his horse swiftly and joined his retinue that was waiting for him at a distance. There, he stopped the horse and pointedly looked at one man in the crowd. The man who understood the chakravarthy's signal approached the chakravarthy and stood attentively in front of him.

'Shatrugnan, are you trained in sculpting?' asked the chakravarthy.

Shatrugnan, without displaying any emotion, said, 'No, my lord.'

'Is that so? You ought to have at least a little training in sculpting. There is no place better than this for this purpose. It is enough if you were to observe Aayanar's disciples.'

'As you wish, my lord. I will begin right away.'

'If someone has joined recently to learn sculpting, you need to observe them too. But they should not notice you.'

When Shatrugnan said, 'As you wish,' his eyebrows were slightly raised.

'Good. If you learn anything new about sculpture, you should inform me in person immediately.'

Speaking thus, the chakravarthy rode away swiftly. The kumara chakravarthy followed him. Unable to keep pace with them, the retinue lagged behind.

Narasimhar had heard parts of the conversation between the chakravarthy and Shatrugnan, and it had confused him. He was already puzzled by the absence of the youth who had wielded the spear at Aayanar's house. When the chakravarthy had ordered the most competent spy in the Pallava kingdom to watch Aayanar's house, not only was Narasimhar surprised but also suspicious. He wanted to ask his father about this. But Mahendrar rode swiftly along the forest path. As Mamallar realized that this indicated that Mahendrar was deep in thought, his curiosity intensified and the speed of his horse accelerated too.

As soon as they crossed the forest, the highway to Mamallapuram was visible. A canal ran along the highway. A column of boats sailed one after the other in that canal towards Kanchi. Most of the boats were laden with sacks of paddy. Each boat was manned by two people.

The trees lining both sides of the highway, the clear water of the canal, the sailing boats, and the lush green lands seen through the trees presented a beautiful sight. At certain places, the shadow of the trees fell on the canal waters and it was a delight to the eyes. At a distance, one of the boatmen sang:

Tell me my beloved parrot! Of the youth
With lips ruby red
Playing divine melodies on his flute.

Tell me my beloved parrot!
Of the youth
With soft countenance
And enchanting smile
Stealing our hearts.

The lilting melody rendered in a tuneful voice wafted on the gentle breeze.

This peace and serenity were deceptive, as thunder, rain, storms and earthquakes were soon to follow. Indicating this, a boat laden with weapons made its way along the canal amidst the vessels filled with paddy. Several weapons like spears, swords, lances, knives and shields filled the boat.

The chakravarthy, who had watched the sight silently thus far, saw the weapon-laden boat and sarcastically remarked, 'Ah! The war preparations in the Pallava kingdom are sound.' He turned and observed his son's face. 'Narasimha! It seems as though you want to ask something.'

'How do you know, appa?' asked the kumara chakravarthy.

'Your face gave it away. Didn't we just discuss abhinayams and facial expressions? Ask what you want,' said the father.

'Where did you send Shatrugnan?'

'To Aayanar's house.'

'Why?'

'Why would a spy be sent? For reconnaissance!'

'What are you saying, father! What is the necessity to snoop around Aayanar's house?'

'We need to be extremely cautious during wartime, Mamalla! During times like these, our enemies' spies may be camouflaged in the ochre robes of monks. There may be treachery within sculptures . . .'

With an uncontrollable shudder, Narasimhar said, 'Ah! What is this? Is Aayanar plotting against us? I am unable to believe this.'

'Did I say Aayanar was plotting against us? That peaceful soul will not hesitate to sacrifice his life for us.'

Mamallar calmed down a little. 'Then what is the necessity of putting his house under surveillance?'

'Our foes' spies may be in that innocent sculptor's house without his knowledge.'

'Spies in Aayanar's house? How did you come to know? I did not observe anyone.'

'Mamallar, rulers should always keep their eyes and ears open. This is extremely essential during wartime. What were your eyes doing when we were in Aayanar's house?' Saying this, the chakravarthy looked at Narasimhar's face.

When Mamallar remembered that he and Sivakami were communicating through their eyes, the kumara chakravarthy's youthful face blushed. At the same time, the boatman's melodious singing was heard at a distance.

Tell me my beloved parrot! What the young lasses claimed of a thief called Kannan,
Is it not their fantasy!
How can a mere butter-stealing child
Speak with his eyes
And steal my heart?
Tell me my beloved parrot!

23

The Royal Hamsam

Looking at an embarrassed Narasimhar, Mahendrar spoke thus. 'Narasimha, it is natural to lose your sight and senses when you view the paintings and sculptures at Aayanar's house. It is the same with me too. As I was slightly doubtful even as we were going to Aayanar's house, I observed keenly . . .'

Narasimhar suppressed his confusion and said, 'What did you observe, father? I did not see anything but paintings and sculptures.'

'Didn't Aayanar's behavior arouse doubts, Narasimha?'

Mamallar did not reply.

'Didn't you observe that he often turned towards the Buddha statue with a worried expression?'

Mamallar's eyes widened.

'Didn't you observe that Aayanar faltered as soon as we neared the Buddha statue?'

Shocked, Narasimhar said, 'Appa, was someone hiding behind the gigantic Buddha statue?'

'Yes, Narasimha! Two people were hiding there! Didn't we meet a bikshu and a youth close to the royal viharam the other night? They were the ones who were hiding.'

'What? Were they hiding behind the Buddha statue at Aayanar's house?'

'Yes, but they have not learnt the art of hiding that well ...'

'How would they know that you possess a third eye, father? I was surprised that you spent so much time at Aayanar's house. Now I understand the reason,' said Narasimhar proudly.

Mahendrar, looking westwards towards the canal, did not respond.

Suddenly, Narasimhar said, 'Appa! I wish to visit Aayanar's house again.'

'Why, Narasimha?'

'I need to return this spear to that youth. Didn't you mention the other night that the spear belonged to the youth who was with the bikshu?'

'I was only guessing the other night; now I am sure. But that youth has no further use for this spear, Narasimha. You may deposit this spear in that boat carrying weapons.'

'Why, father?'

'Paranjyothi is going to learn sculpting from Aayanar; he doesn't require a spear.'

'Paranjyothi, Paranjyothi! What a divine name. I was desirous of befriending that brave youth.'

'I never said that your wish will not be fulfilled!'

'How will it be fulfilled? Is it possible to befriend our enemies' spies?'

'I never said that youth was a spy.'

'Then why was he hiding?'

'That youth is innocent. I believe that deceptive bikshu is using that youth to engage in treachery. I think that the bikshu is an extremely clever spy of the Vatapi kingdom.'

'Appa, sometimes your laidback approach surprises me.'

'What are you referring to, Narasimha?'

'You doubted the bikshu the other night. Why did you not imprison him immediately? Why are you watching him roam around scot-free?'

'Had I imprisoned him the other night, I would not have come to know of the great danger that could have befallen the Pallava empire.'

An excited Narasimhar echoed, 'Great danger?' and looked at Mahendrar.

'Yes, we saw the bikshu and that youth the other night. The following morning, they were not to be seen at the royal viharam. We did not know through which fort gate they had left.'

'Yes!'

'We were surprised that they had mysteriously disappeared.'

'Yes, father!'

'I suspected the fort may have a secret exit, whose location I unravelled some time ago.'

'Did you ride the horse so swiftly because you were thinking of it?'

The chakravarthy kept quiet.

'Where is the secret route, father?'

'We need to look behind the Buddha statue at the royal viharam, Narasimha.'

Narasimhar was stunned by the chakravarthy's intuitive intelligence. He looked towards the west when Mahendrar said, 'There is the royal hamsam.' Three boats were sailing in the canal from Kanchi. The middle boat was white and shaped like a hamsam, a swan. On one side of the boat was a white canopy beneath which was placed a golden throne that glowed brightly. The flag of the Pallava empire, bearing the emblem of a rishabha, a bull, was fluttering majestically atop the mast.

There was no one but the boatmen in the first boat and in the royal boat. Several people were seated in the last boat.

'Ah! The ministers' council has also come. Did you ask them to come?' said Narasimhar.

'Yes. Today the ministers' council is to meet at the port. Before that, I need to inform you of a few things. You must also give me your word,' said Mahendrar.

Narasimhar was taken aback. A muhurtham had passed since the love of his life, Sivakami, had asked him for his word at the lotus pond. Now, it was his idol—his father.

As Mamallar was thinking thus, the three boats neared them.

24

The Promise

The chakravarthy's retinue, which was travelling by foot, had reached the banks of the canal by now.

The members of the ministers' council majestically cheered thus: 'Long live the great king, the chakravarthy of the three realms, the virtuous Mahendra Pallavar!'

Those on the banks of the canal hailed: 'Long live the great king, the vanquisher of foes, the unique seer, the author of *Matha Vilasam*, the tiger amongst artists, the virtuous Mahendra Pallavar!'

The cheer 'Long live the kumara chakravarthy Mamallar!' rose from both sides and reached the skies. The sound of conches and trumpets deafened the ear. The din of drums reverberated in all directions.

The soldiers who had followed Mahendra Varma Pallavar seated themselves in the first of the three boats.

The chakravarthy and the kumara chakravarthy handed over their horses to the attendants, boarded the royal hamsam and sat on the golden throne beneath the white canopy.

The boats sailed towards the port.

When the musical instruments ceased playing, the chakravarthy told his son, 'Narasimha, you must be puzzled that I am seeking a promise from you. It is only fair that you did not respond immediately. You should not commit to anything without knowing is implications. Those who rule a kingdom should be extremely cautious about this.'

'I did not hesitate on that count, father! What is the necessity for you to seek a promise from me? Isn't it enough if you command me? Have I ever acted against your wishes?'

The kumara chakravarthy was earnest about what he said; his voice trembled with emotion.

Since Mahendrar was also overcome by emotion, he remained silent for some time. Then he said, 'Pallava Simha, I know you will carry out the most unpleasant of my orders. However, considering the importance of the matter, I need you to give me your word. Before that I need to inform you of important matters. Day after tomorrow, I am travelling northwards to the battlefront. I do not know when I will return . . .'

'Appa! What are you saying? Are you proceeding to the battlefront leaving me here?' asked an angry Mamallar.

When the chakravarthy said, 'First, I will tell you what I have to, Narasimha. Then you may pose questions,' Narasimhar fell silent.

Mahendrar then said, 'This ancient Pallava dynasty has not engaged in war for long. Twenty-five years ago, I assumed charge of this kingdom. Since then, there has been no war. No major war occurred during the rule of my father, King Simha

Vishnu. At the beginning of his reign, he decimated the Kallapal dynasty, which proved to be a thorn in the relationship between the Cholas and Pandyas, and instated the Cholas on the Uraiyur throne. Since then, the Pallava army has been idle. For the first time, there is war during my lifetime. I am going to request the ministers' council for permission to conduct this war according to my wishes. You too should permit me to do so. Let me bear the responsibility for the outcome of this war, be it victory or defeat. You need not have a share in this . . .'

Narasimhar, who had been patiently listening till now, interrupted saying, 'Appa! Why do you even utter the word defeat? Don't we either attain victory or embrace death bravely on the battlefield? How can I not have a share in this?'

'You have uttered words befitting a descendant of the valiant Pallava dynasty, Narasimha. Victory or death is our dynasty's philosophy. But it is not necessary for both of us to embrace death at the same time. Shouldn't one person be alive to set right the mistake committed by the other? Shouldn't one person be alive to avenge the other?'

'Appa, there has been some very bad news from the warfront. Hence these despondent words.'

'Yes, my child. We have received bad news. The Gangapadi army has surrendered to Pulikesi. The Vatapi army is advancing towards north Pennai.'

'Is that all, father? This is expected from that coward, Durvineethan. Isn't our army from the northern provinces in a state of readiness on the banks of north Pennai? Isn't my uncle coming from Vengi along with a large army?'

'The Vengi army will not come to our aid, Narasimha. Pulikesi's brother, Vishnuvardhanan, is heading towards Vengi with a massive army.'

'Ah! Is the Vatapi army so large? Why didn't we . . .' Mamallar stopped midway. Disappointment was evident in his voice.

'That's my mistake, Narasimha. I did not anticipate such a war during my lifetime. I spent the time I ought to have spent on warfare in dance, music, sculpture and painting . . .'

'So what, father? Didn't Aayanar say this some time ago? Several emperors have emerged and disappeared in this world. People have forgotten their names. But the world will never forget you.'

'But, should we lose this war, the beautiful sculptures at Mamallapuram will serve as a permanent symbol of our disgrace.'

'Never! What you say will happen only if we are alive even after losing the war. The world will blame and ridicule us only if we flee the battlefield. Why should we be concerned about disgrace and blame when we are ready to embrace death?' asked a furious Mamallar.

'Ultimately, we can bravely embrace death on the battlefield. But before that, shouldn't we try to rout our enemies and hoist the flag of victory? That is not an unattainable feat. We only need time. The Vatapi king is well-versed in the art of warfare. But there is no doubt we will defeat him and emerge victorious. I need your full cooperation for this. You should obey me, irrespective of whether you like my commands or not . . .'

Narasimhar said in a very emotional voice, 'Appa, do you have to ask me for help? You are not only my father, but also the ruler with all rights over my body, belongings and soul. You are the premier commander of the Pallava army, empowered to order me to do anything. I am prepared to comply with the harshest of your commands.'

Mahendrar remained silent. The port was visible at a distance towards the east. Flags bearing the bull symbol hoisted on the ships fluttered majestically, covering the sky. Slightly towards the south, the sprawling hills of Mamallapuram were visible.

Mahendrar, who had been attentively watching that sight for some time, turned with a start to Narasimhar and said, 'Narasimha, didn't I tell you that I was proceeding to the battlefield day after tomorrow? I am confident that I will return to view the completed sculptures at Mamallapuram.'

As Narasimhar was silent, Mahendrar spoke further: 'In the event of my not returning, you should continue with these sculptures and ensure they are completed.'

'Was this the promise you sought from me?' asked Mamallar in a curt tone, which betrayed anger and disgust.

'No, not this. If I do not return from the battlefield, you should seek revenge. You should wipe away the disgrace the Pallava empire faced on account of Pulikesi's invasion.'

'Isn't that my duty? Is a promise required to fulfil one's duty?'

'My son! To seek revenge, you should carefully protect your life.'

Narasimhar kept quiet, anxious. He anticipated that more was to come.

'My child, the Pallava lineage that has not been broken for the last five hundred years is now solely dependent on you for continuance. This is the promise I seek from you. You must remain in the Kanchi fort till I return, or till you know for certain that I will not return. You should not leave the fort for any reason. Place your hand in mine and make this promise.' So saying, Mahendrar extended his right hand.

Narasimhar touched Mahendrar's extended hand and said, 'As you wish, father! I will not leave the Kanchi fort till you return.'

Suddenly, the roar of waves was heard at a distance. Several thoughts rose and receded like those waves within Mamallar.

25

The Child the Sea Bestowed

Several thousand years ago, Kanchi's ancient ruling dynasty came to an end without an heir.

The elders in the country fretted, saying, 'A kingdom without a king will be ruined. The subjects will experience untold sorrow in the absence of a monarch.'

Then a great seer told the people, 'Don't worry; I envisioned the sea granting Kanchi a king.'

From then on, sentries were posted on the seashore in that country.

One day, a ship came to the sea coast. The antecedents of the ship were unknown. Even as those on the coast watched, severe cyclonic winds blew. The sea was so tempestuous that onlookers wondered if apocalypse was imminent. The ship rocked to and fro and its masts were destroyed.

Ah! What a calamity! The ship was spinning like the wooden stick used to churn yoghurt. After spinning for some time, the ship capsized. The bellowing of the cyclonic winds and the cries of those aboard the ship were heard in unison.

As soon as the ship sank, the wind ceased blowing. Those who had passively watched from the coast now sprang to action. Boats and catamarans were pushed into the sea. Boatmen and fishermen rushed to rescue those thrown into the sea.

One among them was lucky. Fortune sought him out. It was good fortune not just for him, but for the country as well! It was good fortune that came about due to the citizens' good deeds!

Did the sun come floating on the waves of the blue sea? No, it was not the sun; it was an infant. The child was tied to a plank of wood with a golden hued cloth. The baby's face was glowing.

Ah! Was that child alive? Yes! The child was alive. When the water from the gentle waves splashed on the child's face, he laughed gleefully.

The boatman eagerly rowed his boat towards that plank of wood. He picked up the child and unfastened the knot. He then hugged the child and the child cried since the hair on the boatman's chest was prickly.

The boatman surveyed the boat. That morning he had brought along a few thondai creepers to fasten goods loaded on the boat.

He formed a bed by bundling those creepers along with the leaves. He plucked the tender shoots at the tips of the creepers and strewed them on the bed. He placed the child on the bed made of tender shoots.

The child smiled slightly at the boatman. The boat sailed fast towards the shore.

Hearing the boatman shout joyously as he neared the shore, the onlookers realized that there was something special in the boat.

When the boat reached the shore, the people on the shore surrounded it.

The great soul who had foreseen this came along. He saw the child and said, 'He is the new king of Kanchi whom I saw in my dream! His descendants will ascend the Kanchi throne and rule for a thousand years.' The people were ecstatic.

The elderly man named the divine child given by the sea 'Illandirayan'. He added, 'As the child lay on a bed made of thondai creepers, he will also be called Thondaiman. The Kanchi kingdom will be called Thondai Mandalam because of him.'

A Sanskrit scholar, seeing the child lay on the tender shoots, christened him 'Pallavarayan'. A Tamil scholar translated the name to 'Pottharayan'.

Poets imaginatively composed beautiful verses about the child the sea had bestowed on them.

When one poet said, 'Do you know why the sea is roaring? The sea is proud of having given birth to Illandirayan,' several waves rose and reverberated in agreement.

Tamil scholars of subsequent generations were unwilling to acknowledge the fact that the child came from the sea. They said, 'The child brought by the sea is actually from the hapless Chola dynasty! A Chola prince crossed the seas and reached an island called Mani Pallavam. He fell in love and married the princess of that land, Peelivalai. A child was born to them. When the prince was returning to his country with his wife and son, the ship met with an accident. The child who escaped from the mishap was the founder of the Pallava dynasty, Thondaiman Illandirayan.'

Sanskrit scholars fabricated the story that the Pallavas were the descendants of Ashwatthama, the son of Drona, who was the guru of the Pandavas.

Today, we cannot say for certain whether these stories are true or figments of the imagination. It is quite possible that the descendants of the Pallava dynasty did not know their origins.

But one thing was certain. The Pallavas were great seafarers. That craving flowed in their veins.

In several islands to the east, the original flag of the Pallavas bearing the rishabha insignia, and later the singham insignia, a lion, fluttered proudly.

During the reign of the Pallavas, marine trade with other countries flourished. Several harbours were built on the east coast to moor ships and to load and unload goods. The foremost harbour was in Mamallapuram.

The sea had made inroads into the land to the north of Mamallapuram, spread southwards, and had almost made an island of Mamallapuram.

Natural harbours that were created in this fashion in the vicinity of Kanchi facilitated the docking of hundreds of ships simultaneously and the loading and unloading of ships.

Before Mahendrar's times, that harbour-island had housed storehouses and customs offices. Boatmen and fishermen lived there.

Mahendra Pallavar housed several government officials and sculptors there. He also built a beautiful seaside palace for the members of the royal family. As his dear son was instrumental in initiating sculpture works in that harbour, he named the new city after his son's title.

The chakravarthy and Mamallar stood at the same spot where they had decided to initiate sculpture works, two days after they had met Aayanar.

26

Stone Temples

Five small hills dotted the vacant landscape in the southern part of the Kadal Mallai island.

Hundreds of sculptors were working on three of those hills. They were sculpting each of the hills into a temple.

The pillars of the front hall of one temple were being chiselled, while the tower of the second temple was being carved. Sculptors had just begun sculpting a temple out of the third hill.

Rows of sheds had been erected to house the sculptors and workmen.

The tall trees and lush green creepers that surrounded Aayanar's forest residence were not seen in this province. The terrain was sandy towards the north. Beyond this, the ebb and flow of the white frothy waves was seen sporadically. Towards the south and the west, small rocks and bushes lay scattered across a great distance.

But the scene towards the north and northwest was very different. There were tall buildings that grazed the sky and slim coconut trees that grew between them. Beyond the buildings, the rishabha flags hoisted atop the masts of hundreds of ships were fluttering in the breeze.

At the centre of the location where the sculpture works were being carried out stood a majestic stone elephant.

The chakravarthy and his son, who came on elephants, alighted and stood near the stone elephant. Attendants held a wide white canopy over them to protect them from the sun.

Mahendra chakravarthy and his son stood at the same spot and in the same fashion as they had seven years ago. But back then, the hills and rocks had been bare.

'Appa! Look at this rock's shadow! Doesn't it look like an elephant?' the heir of the Pallava dynasty, Narasimha Varman, had asked all those years back.

The chakravarthy had looked at the shadow Narasimha Varman was pointing out.

'Ah!' he exclaimed in surprise. Several indescribable emotions resonated in that exclamation.

Mahendrar was immersed in deep thought and lost consciousness of the outside world for some time. Then he hugged Narasimhar and said, 'My child! You have discovered and articulated an amazing fact. You do not realize the worth of your words.'

Narasimha, who was twelve years old then, continued even more enthusiastically. 'Appa, doesn't the shadow of that hill resemble a temple?'

'Yes, Narasimha. Yes. The shadow of that hill does resemble a temple. We will make a temple out of it. We will make five temples out of these five hills. We will create an elephant, a lion and Nandi out of the smaller rocks. We will convert this harbour into a dream world. We will create sculptures that will astound the people who visit this harbour even after a thousand years,' announced Mahendrar.

Soon, several sculptors armed with their tools arrived in that province. They began working on the hills and rocks. A place which had been calm till then resounded with the *kal kal* sound of the chisels wielded by hundreds of sculptors.

Hearing the noise, the tiny rabbits that lived in the bushes came out. With raised ears, they watched what was going on. They then fled that place.

The sculpting which had begun then continued to this date. The chakravarthy and Mamallar stood at the same place close to the rocks that had assumed the forms of an elephant, a lion and a bull.

'Narasimha, for various reasons I am happy that the war is about to occur at the current juncture. But I am worried that the work on the stone temples may be interrupted and that these works may not be completed during my lifetime. Do you know about the annual festival that Harshavardhana conducts at Kanyakubja in the north, Narasimha?'

'I know, father. He has built three temples for Lord Shiva, Lord Suryanarayana and Lord Buddha. There are annual festivals in all the three temples. I have heard that citizens belonging to all three faiths congregate and celebrate at the same time.'

'Mamallar, Harshavardhana rules a kingdom which is larger than the Pallava empire. His wealth is far greater than ours. His fame has spread all over the world. But if my intention is fulfilled, the Pallava dynasty will attain glory that far exceeds Harsha's and any other ruler who has reigned over Bharata. The temples constructed by Harsha are made of bricks and wood. They will be destroyed in a hundred years. But these stone temples cannot be destroyed . . .'

'Which deities are you going to install in these temples, father? These five temples are meant for Lord Shiva, Goddess Parvati, Vinayakar, Subramaniar and Chandikeshwarar, aren't they?'

'No, Narasimha! My action will surpass Harshavardhana's. I am going to dedicate four temples to the four religions widely practiced in Tamil Nadu. One temple will be consecrated for Lord Shiva and Goddess Parvati. The second temple will be dedicated to Mahavishnu and Mahalakshmi. A gigantic statue of Lord Buddha will adorn the third temple. The founder of Jainism, Vardhaman Mahaveera, will be deified in the fourth temple.'

Mamallar's amazement and pride was evident when he exclaimed, 'Ha!'

'Yes, Narasimha. The actual reason for my renouncing Jainism and embracing Saivism was to bring about religious tolerance in our kingdom. Saivism treats all other religions equally and allows the honoring of other religions. Other religions do not allow this. I converted to Saivism for this reason. I wanted to treat and honor all four religions in our kingdom. To demonstrate this, I am waiting for the wrath of the Buddhists and Jains to subside. Before that, the Jain monks hastily ruined everything . . .'

'What did the Jain monks ruin?'

'Yes, they are the cause of this war. The Jain monks who left Kanchi and dispersed in all four directions did not keep quiet. Do you know who crowned the father of Gangapadi Durvineethan? It was your grandfather, King Simha Vishnu. Durvineethan has now aligned himself with our arch foe, the Chalukya king. I heard that the Jain poet, Ravikeerthi, and Durvineethan's guru, Pujyapathar, are with Pulikesi's army. They are accompanying the army. If monks who have renounced the world, especially Jain monks who practise non-violence, come to the battlefield, how angry must they be with me?'

'Why do you need to worry about that, father? Let all the Jain monks and bikshus join our enemies. By the grace of the three-eyed Lord Shiva and the chakra-wielding Tirumal, we will win.'

'I am not worried about victory and defeat. I regret that there will be obstacles in attaining my goals.' The chakravarthy's voice betrayed the sorrow he felt as he spoke.

Mamallar kept quiet for some time and then asked, 'To which god do you intend dedicating the fifth temple?'

'It seems a new religion has been established overseas. People say that the founder of this religion is Jesus Christ. I do not know anything about that new religion. I was thinking of installing the deity of that new religion, as soon as I come to know the details. But doesn't all that seem to be a fantasy now?'

Mamallar, who was astonished at Mahendrar's intentions, asked, 'Why should it be a fantasy? Why should sculpting be disrupted by war?'

'I hope there is no disruption. I hope that these five temples will be completed by the time the war is over. That's why I have asked Aayanar to come here today . . . The work is progressing at a relaxed pace since he is residing in the middle of the forest. I am going to ask him to stay here and complete the work expeditiously . . . There, Aayanar has come . . .'

Narasimhar looked around eagerly. Aayanar was looking out from one side of a palanquin. A vision similar to the full moon, glowing in broad daylight, was visible on the other side. Should it be mentioned that the full moon was Sivakami's face? Narasimhar's wish was fulfilled.

27

A Horse

The palanquin bearers lowered the palanquin to the ground as soon as they saw the Pallava chakravarthy and his son. Aayanar and Sivakami stepped out of the palanquin and walked reverentially towards them.

'Aayanar! Please come! It is good you brought Sivakami along. Was the journey comfortable?' enquired the chakravarthy.

'How else can it be in your regime, Pallavendra?' Aayanar said as he approached the chakravarthy.

Sivakami, who followed Aayanar demurely, also prostrated before the chakravarthy. Her heart was filled with reverence and respect for the chakravarthy. At the same time, she also felt an inexpressible fear.

'Sivakami, may all fortune be bestowed upon you. May the art of Bharatanatyam, which has sought refuge in you, flourish further and attain totality,' blessed Mahendra Pallavar. He then started talking with Aayanar.

'Aayanar, didn't you say that your trip was comfortable today? One cannot be certain it will be this way going forward. There will be considerable troop movement on the rods till this war is over. So it will be good if you reside here for some time . . .'

Aayanar was taken aback. Images of the incomplete sculptures of dance postures at his forest house flitted before his eyes.

He started saying, 'Pallavendra—'

Mahendrar said firmly, 'Do not argue. You and your daughter relocate here tomorrow. This is my command.'

A trembling Aayanar said, 'Pallavendra. Why would I disobey your command? I will do as you say.'

'These temples must be completed as soon as possible. You need not attend to any other work till the temples are complete. I have ordered the treasury in-charge to give you as much money as you require and as often as you need for these works. I have also arranged for more workmen to assist you. If there is an interruption for any reason, you may inform the kumara chakravarthy.' When the chakravarthy said this, Aayanar looked at the kumara chakravarthy.

'Yes, Aayanar! For some time you should intimate your requirements to Narasimhar. Tomorrow I am leaving for the battlefield with the Pallava army. The ministers' council has granted Narasimhar the right to administrate the kingdom and all other responsibilities. From tomorrow, Narasimhar is the chakravarthy,' said Mahendra Pallavar.

Sivakami had been worried and scared when she heard the chakravarthy speak so firmly. But when she heard his final words, she was exultant. Her mind was filled with joyous thoughts. Foremost amongst these thoughts was the fact that Mamallar was not going to the battlefield. Also, he would have all the powers due to the chakravarthy. Henceforth, there would be no curbs to their meeting often. Sivakami day-dreamed about conversing freely with Mamallar on the banks of the lotus pond. She looked at Mamallar affectionately from the corner of her eye. But what was this? Why was there a scowl on his gentle face? Why was he not looking at her? Perhaps he did not like her coming to this place.

Sivakami eagerly looked at Mamallar twice or thrice. He did not even glance in her direction. Yesterday, by the lotus pond, he had eyed her as though he wanted to devour her. When the chakravarthy and Aayanar were conversing at her house, he had communicated secrets through his eyes. Now, what was the reason for him not wanting to look at her? Tears were about to fill Sivakami's eyes. She quickly went and stood behind a rock.

But what was Narasimhar's true state of mind? Yes, he was angry. But we know the person towards whom the anger was directed. When Narasimhar himself could not decipher his feelings, how could Sivakami be aware?

Mamallar's heart was brimming with love for Sivakami. Seeing her divine face look out of the palanquin, he was jubilant. He was eager to welcome her and hold her hand to help her get down from the palanquin. As all this was not possible, his affection transformed into anger. That anger was directed towards everything and everyone. He was angry with his status as the kumara chakravarthy of a large kingdom. 'Why did I have to be born at the chakravarthy's palace? Why was I not born as a humble sculptor's son?' he thought.

When his father mentioned that he was not going to war, the slight smile on Sivakami's face further fanned his anger. She did not realize that his being at the palace without heading to the battlefield was shameful. Since he was not at the warfront, would it be possible to meet her often? No. His father had made him promise that he would not leave the Kanchi fort. Being unaware of all this, Sivakami was beaming with happiness.

Such thoughts intensified Narasimhar's anger.

While Mamallar and Sivakami were consumed by their own thoughts, the chakravarthy and Aayanar continued with their conversation.

As they were talking, the chakravarthy observed that Aayanar alternated between looking at him and Mamallar. He enquired, 'Aayanar, do you have a request to make? Is there anything you wish to inform Narasimhar or me?'

Aayanar hesitantly replied, 'Yes, Pallavendra. I require a horse.'

'What did you ask for?'

'I need a high-breed horse.'

'Horse? Did you ask for a horse? You could have asked for my life or this Pallava kingdom instead! Don't you know we are facing a major war of a scale Dakshina Bharata has not witnessed before? Don't you know that several emissaries have to travel in all directions from Kanchi every day? Ask for anything but a horse!' thundered the chakravarthy.

As Aayanar had not witnessed Mahendra Pallavar speak so agitatedly before, he was stunned.

'Oh! It seems you don't require anything but a horse. A great sculptor of the Pallava empire is entreating me for a horse. I do not want to bear the blame of not acceding to your request. I will provide you with a horse. But please tell me why you require a horse. Don't you and Sivakami have a palanquin and the bearers to travel? Then why do you require a horse?' asked the chakravarthy.

Aayanar mustered courage to say, 'Pallavendra, I requested a horse for a very important task. But if war preparations will be affected . . .' and then paused.

'What is that important task? May I know? Or is it a secret, Aayanar?'

'My lord! It is a secret. But not something you should not know. Haven't we discussed several times that we should unravel the secret of the colour paintings in Ajantha? A person who knows the secret of the paints is currently at the Buddha sangramam of Nagarjuna mountain . . .'

'Why didn't you mention this before, Aayanar? I wouldn't have objected to it if it was such an important task. I once thought of befriending Pulikesi so that I could view the wonderful paintings at Ajantha. All that is now a dream. Never mind, I will definitely provide a horse. Aayanar, will a horse suffice or do you require anything else?'

'I require your travel permit with the rishabha insignia embossed as this is wartime.'

'I will give that too. Whom are you proposing to send for such an important task? Perhaps you intend going there?'

'I don't even know how to mount a horse, my lord! I will send a disciple of mine.'

'He will have to travel through the route by which our foe's army is approaching. He will have to carry a good weapon. Please give him this spear before sending him.' So saying, the chakravarthy extended the spear he had taken from Narasimhar.

As Aayanar hesitated, Chakravarthy said, 'Why the reluctance? This spear belongs to the youth you propose to send. It is the weapon that rescued you and Sivakami from the wrath of the mad elephant. Paranjyothi will not object to accepting it.'

Hearing this, not only Aayanar, but also Narasimhar and Sivakami were astounded.

Aayanar fumbled when he asked, 'Pallavendra, how did you know?'

'Lord Buddha told me in my dreams! He also told me about those who were hiding behind his statue at your house the other day. Aayanar, don't you know: nothing happens in the Pallava empire without reaching the eyes and ears of the Pallava chakravarthy?'

Immediately Aayanar folded his hands and said in a choked voice, 'Pallavendra! Please forgive me if I have done anything wrong. I undertook this task out of my love for painting.'

'Respected sculptor, I am as keen as you are to know the secret of the Ajantha paintings. Please send Paranjyothi by all means. But do not tell that bikshu that I am aware of this mission. I don't know why Buddhists doubt me. They do not understand my devotion to Lord Buddha. Aayanar, in one of the five temples carved out of the hills, I am going to install a gigantic statue of Lord Buddha. I was talking about this to Narasimhar when you arrived,' stated the chakravarthy.

Several thoughts rose like waves within Sivakami, who was standing unseen beside a rock and listening to this interesting conversation.

'This chakravarthy is so smart. I thought of warning Mamallar about the bikshu, but he already knows everything. It seems to be impossible to hide anything from him. Does he also know our secret? Is that why the kumara chakravarthy is ignoring me? Have we committed any mistake?' These thoughts saddened her. It was evident that she would not be at peace if she did not meet the kumara chakravarthy and ascertain the reason for his anger.

Her sight fell on an ochre stone lying on the ground. Immediately, an idea struck her. She picked up the stone and drew a picture on the rock.

She drew a wave-like line to signify water in the pond. She then drew a lotus above that line and two lotus buds adjacent to the lotus. She also drew the picture of a fawn on the banks of the pond.

As she was drawing, she realized that Narasimha Varmar was observing her from the corner of his eye.

When Sivakami completed drawing the picture, she regained her composure. Narasimha Varmar would definitely understand the message in the picture. The picture would be meaningless to others. If the kumara chakravarthy's affection for her was genuine, he would definitely come to the lotus pond.

That evening, Mahendrar and Narasimhar were returning to Kanchi on horseback. The rock on which Sivakami had sketched the lotus pond lay en route. Narasimhar dismounted from the horse the instant they reached the rock. When he saw the picture, his face bloomed like a lotus. He picked up that same ochre stone and drew a spear between the fawn and the lotus.

28

On the Mountain Track

Four days after Aayanar arranged for the high-breed horse, Paranjyothi, dressed like a warrior, was riding down the mountain road all by himself.

Sunset was just two nazhigai away. Nevertheless, the evening sun in that mountainous region singed his right cheek.

Paranjyothi, who had ridden all morning in the scorching sun, was exhausted; the horse was also fatigued. So, he rode slowly.

The horse ascended the mountain path at a snail's pace. Paranjyothi's mind traveled back in time. His incredible experiences during the last one week flashed repeatedly through his mind.

Paranjyothi wondered if the incidents that had occurred ever since he arrived at Kanchi accompanied by the bikshu were a reality or a fantasy. He was even amazed that the rustic boy who had left Thirusengattankudi by foot twelve days ago, was now riding a high-breed horse.

The sweltering heat made him recall the beauty and comforts of Tamil Nadu's roads. In the Chola and Pallava kingdoms, the dense foliage along the large roads provided cool shade. On both sides of the road, lush green paddy swayed in the gentle breeze. Mature crop bent under the weight of the grain. Verdant coconut and mango groves at various places were a feast to the eyes. The very sight of banana and sugarcane fields quenched travellers' thirst.

Yes, suffering from thirst during a journey was unheard of. There were countless ponds with lotuses, hyacinths and water lilies growing on them. The highways were interspersed with rivers, brooks and small canals. The sight of small canals with water flowing in them and green plants and creepers growing on both sides was beautiful. Also pleasing was the sight of dry canal beds. The joy of walking on the sands of a dry canal was unimaginable. While walking on the canal bed, the fragrance from the wild jasmine creepers growing on both banks was exhilarating.

Equally joyful was the experience of travelling on a highway flanked by fully grown banyan trees and neem trees, at noon. In the month of Pankuni, new banyan sprouts glowed. Neem trees were filled with blossoms. How can the beauty of the tender mango sprouts be described? One day, the mango tree would be covered with dark blue tender sprouts. The next day the sprouts would have assumed a soft shade of red. The day after, they would be golden-hued.

To praise the Lord who had bestowed such natural beauty, the branches of trees would sway in the breeze and cuckoos would sing incessantly.

Paranjyothi, who had seen similar sights while travelling to Kanchi from Thirusengattankudi, had neither appreciated their beauty nor experienced the pleasure of them.

Now, bare hills met the eye everywhere. He was travelling on an arid route devoid of greenery. Frequently recollecting the farms and groves of Chola Mandalam and the dams and forests of Thondai Mandalam made him happy.

* * *

As the sun was setting behind the mountains in the west, Paranjyothi turned a bend in that mountainous region and a rare sight awaited him, who had seen just thorny bushes and spurge plants the whole day. Thousands of purasa trees of varying heights covered a vast area. The scene was filled with flowers with no leaves visible. The flowers were blood red and grew in bunches. The red rays of the evening sun accentuated the redness of the flowers.

It was a rare and beautiful sight, but it was also unnerving. In the southwest corner of Paranjyothi's native village Sengattankudi was a graveyard in which a few purasa trees grew. During the months of Pankuni and Cittirai, he had observed the red flowers covering the tree. Hence he associated purasa trees in full bloom with the graveyard.

Now, when he was far away from his village, travelling all by himself through a forest path, he was reminded of the graveyard. This instilled a deep sense of fear in him. Along with the recollection of the graveyard came thoughts of ghosts and apparitions. Though Paranjyothi was intrinsically brave, he was very scared of ghosts and apparitions. The idea of travelling through the forest in the dark caused his heart to skip a beat and his stomach to churn. He knew that the rest house where he was to spend the night was at the intersection of two mountains. He knew he would reach there only a jaamam after darkness set in. Considering the lunar phase, the earlier part of the night was bound to be dark. 'Oh no! Why did I delay en route?' Thinking thus, Paranjyothi tried to spur the horse to go faster. But how fast could the horse, which had travelled all day, go?

That eerie mountainous region did instill fear. Here was not an animal or bird in sight. With the onset of darkness, foxes would start howling, heightening the horror.

The previous day, Paranjyothi had travelled northwards on the wide highway. There was plenty of human and horse movement. He was stopped several times on the way. He had to show the travel permit the chakravarthy had issued and then proceed.

Today, when he departed from the highway and turned to the mountain road, there was no such problem. But now Paranjyothi wished that a large retinue of horses would traverse that route.

Ah! What was that noise? It sounded like horse hooves. Yes, a horse was coming from behind. Who could I be? It would be good, no matter who it was. Wouldn't he have a companion to travel with in the dark?

Was only one horse coming? Or were there many? Paranjyothi stopped his horse and listened intently. Suddenly, the noise stopped. Was it just a figment of his imagination? Was it a result of his desire for company?

Paranjyothi rode his horse further. Again he heard the sound of a horse approaching from behind. When he turned around, nothing was visible. Since the mountain path was serpentine, it would not have been possible to see a horse even if it was close by.

By then, the sun had set and darkness was enveloping the region.

When Paranjyothi reached that part of the road which did not have too many turns, he accelerated the pace of his riding slightly for some time, stopped abruptly, and looked around. He saw a horse coming at a distance and a man mounted on the horse. When Paranjyothi's horse stopped, that man halted his horse too.

Paranjyothi was enraged. He skilfully turned his horse around and swiftly rode towards the horse standing behind him. Twilight had set in.

29

Travel Companion

When Paranjyothi turned around and rode towards the horse standing behind him, all his fear had transformed into anger. The spear he held in his hand was aloft, ready to be flung at the chest of the rider of the horse behind him.

But as soon as Paranjyothi approached the horse, the rider's actions rendered the wielding of the spear unnecessary.

That well-built man sporting a large moustache and turban jumped off his horse screaming, 'Aiyayo! Aiyayo! Ghost! Ghost!' Seeing this, Paranjyothi's fear and anger dissipated and he burst out laughing. The fact that the man who fell down was dressed like a warrior with a large sword fastened to his waist, made him laugh even more. He was slightly placated by the thought that he was not the only one who feared ghosts and spirits.

The man who fell down shrieked, 'Aiyayo! The ghost is laughing! I am scared!'

Paranjyothi, who wanted to have some more fun, poked the man slightly with his spear and proclaimed in a deep voice, 'I will not spare you! I will gobble you up!'

The next moment, something which Paranjyothi had not anticipated happened. He was unable to understand what it was at that moment. He felt that he was falling upside down into a pit. Immediately, it felt as though a thousand bolts of lightning had struck his head. Subsequently, the Vindhya mountain sat on his chest. Then a terrible apparition shook his shoulders laughing, 'Ha, ha, ha!'

Only when Paranjyothi had composed himself and could think clearly did he understand what had happened.

When Paranjyothi touched the fallen man's hand with the tip of his spear and threatened, 'I will gobble you!' that man had held Paranjyothi's spear firmly and tugged at it. Paranjyothi fell headlong from the horse with a thud. Immediately, that man leapt up like lightning, sat on Paranjyothi's chest and shook his shoulders. He then laughed and said loudly, 'Ha, ha, ha! You are not a ghost, you're only a man! You just tried to scare me by screaming like a ghost. How amusing! Ha, ha, ha!' He then got off Paranjyothi's chest and also lifted Paranjyothi from the ground. That man placed his arm around Paranjyothi's shoulders as though he knew him well and asked amicably, 'Thambi! I was scared to travel through this ghastly place all alone. Fortunately, I now have a travel companion. Where are you going, thambi?'

Paranjyothi was shocked by the incident. He felt very angry and ashamed as well. He realized that the person who had scared him thus was no ordinary man; he was a strong and valiant person. So, he also felt respect for him.

But when that man asked, 'Where are you going, thambi?' he remembered the bikshu's words of caution.

He shrugged that man's hand off his shoulder and asked in a hostile tone, 'How does it matter to you where I am going?'

'It does not matter to me, appa! Not at all. It is enough that tonight you will be my travel companion. It may be a confidential task. But . . .'

That warrior paused after saying this and looked at Paranjyothi intently. Before Paranjyothi could understand the implication of that look, he had fallen down again. Not only did that warrior push Paranjyothi down, he also sat next to him and started strangling him.

'Aren't you a spy from Vatapi? Tell me the truth,' questioned the man in a harsh tone.

Tears almost filled Paranjyothi's eyes, out of anger and shame. He said in a choked voice, 'Are you a true warrior? If you are, stand face to face with me! Engage in a duel with me!'

'Do I have to fight with you? Why, appane? If you are a spy from Vatapi, I will send you to Yama Loka right away. If you are not a spy, why fight with you? We can then be friends. You just prove that you're not a spy. Do you possess a rishabha insignia like this?' As he was talking, that warrior used his right hand to remove a square piece of copper fastened to his waist. It was the travel permit given to the Pallava king's emissaries.

When Paranjyothi reluctantly showed the warrior his travel permit, he not only helped Paranjyothi stand up, but also hugged him affectionately. 'Thambi, forgive me. Your physiognomy indicates that you can never be our adversaries' spy. But as this is wartime, no one can be trusted. Good, get on to your horse. We'll talk as we ride!' Speaking thus, the warrior very adroitly leapt on to his horse.

Paranjyothi murmured to himself as he mounted the horse, 'What is the necessity to talk to him? After crossing this mountain path, he should be taught a lesson.'

Evening was fading into night with accompanying darkness. Stars were sparkling like diamonds in the sky. The two men started riding together in the dim light.

30

Mayurasanman

Silence prevailed in that mountain forest. The only sound heard was that of horse hooves.

Both the travellers kept quiet.

Several thoughts occurred to Paranjyothi. Who could this person sporting a large moustache and massive turban riding next to him be? There was no doubt that he was proficient in warfare. That man had harassed Paranjyothi so much within a short span of time. When Paranjyothi recollected the man pulling him down from the horse, sitting on his chest like a mountain, pushing him down again when he had least expected it and strangling him with his iron-like hands, he was extremely angry. At the same time, the skill, strength and astuteness he had demonstrated in his actions instilled respect and reverence. Ah! How fortunate would he be if he could establish long-lasting friendship with such a great warrior!

This warrior was such a contrast to the bikshu he had befriended while travelling from Thirusengattankudi to

Kanchi. The bikshu had spoken to him affectionately and had helped him a lot. But what was the reason for the bikshu not commanding the kind of respect and admiration the man who pinned him down did?

At the same time, he remembered the bikshu's warning when he embarked on the journey. 'Do not trust anyone whom you meet on the way! Even if he is friendly, do not divulge your destination or that you are carrying a message. There are several people besides Aayanar desirous of learning the secret of Ajantha's indelible paints. They will not hesitate to kill you to obtain this. So you keep the purpose of your visit extremely confidential. To extract this information from you, people may employ several ruses. But you should not get duped . . .'

Recollecting the bikshu's words, Paranjyothi felt that his co-traveller could be one such person. Was it to extract the message given by the bikshu that he had pushed him down from the horse and badgered him so much?

The sound of a fox howling in a fearsome but mournful tone was heard at a distance. The next moment, several foxes started howling in response. Paranjyothi shivered and perspired out of fear. When one group of foxes stopped howling, another group started. When the hills echoed with the sound of the foxes howling, that region became indescribably eerie.

The warrior who had been travelling silently thus far said, 'Thambi, how courageous of you to travel all alone in this mountainous region during twilight. I have travelled by myself several times. Even I felt unsettled in this region some time ago.'

Paranjyothi then responded hesitantly, 'Aiyya, when you saw me, didn't you fall from the horse screaming, "Ghost! Ghost!"? Why was that? Were you genuinely scared? Or did you pretend to be scared to push me down? You, who screamed so hysterically just a short time ago, don't seem to display an iota of fear now!'

'Ah! Don't you know that? As long as one is alone, he cannot counter even one ghost. The ghost will assault the lone man and kill him. But if two men join hands, two hundred ghosts can be chased away! I have heard that, in this mountainous region, two hundred thousand ghosts roam around during the night shrieking, "Ho, ho!" Even if all the ghosts were to come together, they will not be able to harm two men. Thambi, do you know the story of this region?' asked the warrior.

'I don't know it. Please tell me,' replied Paranjyothi.

The story that the warrior narrated was as follows:

Almost two hundred and fifty years ago, a Brahmin named Veerasanman, accompanied by his young disciple Mayurasanman, came to Kanchi from Utthara Bharata. They were already well-versed in the scriptures. In those days, only when a great scholar of the Kanchi University confirmed a candidate's scholarly proficiency was his education considered complete. Veerasanman and Mayurasanman came to Kanchi for this purpose. One day, as they were walking down one of Kanchi's royal thoroughfares, they encountered the Pallava king's horsemen. As the guru and sishya were deeply engaged in an important debate, they did not give way to the horsemen. This enraged one of the horsemen who kicked Veerasanman. As the sishya was unable to tolerate his guru being insulted, he grabbed that horseman's sword and wielded it. The injured horseman fell down. The other horsemen tried to capture Mayurasanman, who realized that his life would be in danger if he was caught. So, Mayurasanman mounted horse that belonged to the fallen warrior, sword in hand, killed the warriors who tried to capture him and fled Kanchi.

Hearing of this incident, which was a shame to the Pallava empire, several horsemen who swore to ensnare

Mayurasanman, pursued him. But they could not capture him. Mayurasanman finally reached Sri Parvatham on the banks of River Krishna. He hid from the Pallava warriors in a dense forest on that mountain. He mobilized the tribals in that region, formed a large army and established an independent kingdom. He then invaded Kanchi to avenge the insult to his guru. Mayurasanman's forces and the Pallava army clashed in this mountainous region. The battle raged continuously for seven days. Thousands of soldiers lost their lives in that fight. The mountains were drenched in blood.

The purasa trees grew after some time on the blood-soaked land. The war had occurred during the month of Pankuni. Every Pankuni thereafter, the purasa trees shed their leaves and crimson flowers bloomed. The residents of the nearby villages believed that the ghosts of the soldiers who lost their lives in the battle still roamed around here. These ghost warriors, mounted on ghost horses, wielding their swords and calling out 'Ho, ho', were said to roam around this uninhabited region. Should a lone traveller pass this way, it was believed that the ghost warriors would kill him and drink his blood to quench their thirst!

Hearing this story, Paranjyothi lost even the slight fear he had felt thus far. He was sure that the stories of ghosts roaming about were mere superstition. He laughingly said, 'When you saw me, did you fall off the horse shrieking thinking I was the ghost of a warrior who died two hundred and fifty years ago?'

'I can fight a flesh-and-blood man. I can fight with the bow and arrow, sword, spear and can also wrestle. But who can fight ghosts?' said that warrior in a slightly harsh tone.

Paranjyothi, in an attempt to change the topic, asked, 'That's all right, aiyya. What was the outcome of the battle fought here? Who won?'

'The Pallava army was thrice as large as Mayurasanman's army. So, the Pallava army won. Mayurasanman was captured and produced before the Pallava king with thirty-six injuries inflicted on his body . . . !'

'What happened after that?' asked Paranjyothi eagerly.

When that warrior said, 'You tell me what happened,' Paranjyothi's curiosity was piqued.

31

Vyjayanthi

Paranjyothi recollected what the bikshu had said about Mayurasanman. But the bikshu's version of the story had not been as interesting. Neither had Paranjyothi liked the bikshu's underlying intent when he related the story. When the bikshu said, 'Perhaps you may become like Mayurasanman one day!' Paranjyothi had been disgusted. He had been put off by the very name Mayurasanman.

But when Paranjyothi came to know of the brave war he had waged and how he had been produced before the Pallava king with thirty-six wounds on his body, his respect for Mayurasanman grew multifold.

'Such a brave warrior would have refused to surrender to the Pallava king. Should a person rebel against the Pallava king, it was customary to bury him up to his shoulders and to have an elephant trample him! The Pallava king must have awarded the same punishment!' said Paranjyothi bitterly.

'No, thambi, never! The kings of Anga, Vanga, Kalinga, Kashmir and Kambhoja would have acted in the manner you described. But the behaviour of the Kanchi kings was different . . .'

'What did the Pallava king do?'

'He forgave Mayurasanman, praised his valour and returned the kingdom he had established. He himself crowned Mayurasanman and returned to Kanchi!'

'Is that so?' asked Paranjyothi, in a tone that revealed his amazement. 'Was Mayurasanman grateful for this?' he asked.

'Not only Mayurasanman, but also the descendants of the Kadamba dynasty he established paid tribute to the Pallavas and remained loyal for two hundred years. They expanded their kingdom between the Krishna and Tungabhadra rivers. After some time, they established their capital at Vyjayanthi Pattinam. They sought assistance from the Pallava kings whenever they were in danger. Don't you know that Pulikesi's uncle invaded the Kadamba kingdom twenty years ago?'

'I didn't know. What was that about?' asked Paranjyothi eagerly.

'Yes, you're a young boy. How would you know? Pulikesi has now assumed a demonic stature and has invaded the Pallava kingdom. But when he and his brothers were young, their uncle, Mangalesan, ruled the Vatapi kingdom. He developed ambitions of conquering other states and becoming a powerful chakravarthy. He crossed River Tungabhadra and entered the Kadamba kingdom. He advanced up to the city of Vyjayanthi and laid siege. Then the Pallava army stationed in the northern province of the Pallava empire came to the rescue of the Kadamba king. A massive war was waged in the vicinity of Vyjayanthi Pattinam.'

'What was the outcome of the war?'

'Why ask? The heroic Pallava army won. The defeated Chalukyas retreated and fled. Ah! If only the Pallava army had pursued and decimated the Chalukyas, there would have been no war now!' stated that warrior.

Paranjyothi was keen to know such ancient history. He was deeply interested in wars, warfare techniques and the outcome of wars. It was also helpful to counter the fatigue of travelling on a new-moon night.

'Why didn't the Pallava army pursue the fleeing Chalukya army?' he asked.

'There were several reasons. The key reason was a casualty that the Pallava army had suffered at the battle near Vyjayanthi Pattinam. The commander of the Pallava army lost his life in that battle!'

Paranjyothi's attention was momentarily diverted.

'Aiyya! What was the name of that brave commander?' he asked.

'Haven't you heard? It was Commander Kalipahai, the uncle of the current commander of the Pallava army . . .'

'I have heard about him. I have also heard about Thilakavathi, that chivalrous man's fiancée,' said Paranjyothi in a reverent tone.

'You know everything! You also seem to be a devout Saivite!' said that warrior.

'Yes, aiyya! My family and friends are all Saivites. I came to Kanchi with the express intention of securing an audience with Thirunavukkarasar . . .' Saying this, Paranjyothi abruptly stopped.

'Is that so, thambi? I too am a Saivite. Did you obtain Thirunavukkarasar's darisanam at Kanchi?'

'No...'

'Why?'

'I had to perform this task before obtaining securing an audience.'

'Which task?'

Paranjyothi composed himself and responded, 'Aiyya, if you don't enquire about my mission, I will not be forced to lie!'

'Ah! You're an intelligent boy!' said that warrior. Then he said, 'Thambi, I have a son just like you. He too is of your age. He insisted on accompanying me on this journey. I forbade him from doing so. So he is angry with me . . .'

Paranjyothi was slightly envious of that fortunate boy who had such a valiant father.

In an attempt to forget that unwanted thought, Paranjyothi said, 'Aiyya, you stopped midway while talking of the Vyjayanthi war. You said that Commander Kalipahayar lost his life in that battle. Didn't another commander assume charge of the Pallava army? Why didn't the Pallava army pursue the vanquished Chalukya army?'

The warrior then raised an irrelevant query, 'Have you seen the Kanchi chakravarthy, one of whose titles is Vichitra Siddhar, thambi?'

Paranjyothi kept quiet.

Nodding appreciatively, the warrior continued, 'Vichitra Siddhar harboured very strange thoughts those days—that there should be no war in the world. He believed that people should be involved in the arts like sculpture and painting and should spend their lives joyfully, singing and dancing. He was content with his kingdom. He also believed that expanding his kingdom was unnecessary. At such a time, when Pulikesi called for truce, he ordered that the war be stopped.'

'When did Pulikesi become king?'

'Mangalesan, Pulikesi's uncle, desirous of ruling the kingdom, imprisoned Pulikesi and his brothers. When Mangalesan was invading Vyjayanthi, Pulikesi and his brothers escaped from prison. Pulikesi ascended the Vatapi throne after killing the vanquished Mangalesan. He immediately sent a message to the Kanchi chakravarthy, calling for a truce. Mahendra chakravarthy accepted the truce, which was akin to making peace with a cobra. He is bearing the venomous consequence of that now.'

'What venomous consequence?'

'What venomous consequence! Don't you know that Pulikesi's army has captured Vyjayanthi and is advancing further? I heard horrific news. When Pulikesi captured Vyjayanthi, he looted the city of all its wealth and ordered that the city be set ablaze. I cannot believe this. If it is true . . .'

'If so . . .'

'If it is true, I would say that Kanchi's Mahendra Varmar deserves this and more. The kings and emperors of the world secure titles like a "lion in battle" and a "tiger in combat". Isn't one of the Kanchi chakravarthy's titles a "tiger among painters"? He deserves this.'

Paranjyothi was again immersed in silence. The news of Vyjayanthi Pattinam being set on fire disturbed him.

After a pause, that warrior said, 'Thambi! I will not ask you where you are going and what your mission is. But do you mind telling me where you intend staying tonight?'

'I understand there is a Mahendra rest house after crossing this mountain. I intend staying there. I thought I could reach it before it was dark.'

'Ah! See the light there! It is from the Mahendra rest house you referred to. I too am staying there tonight,' said that warrior.

32

Kumbakarnan

When the two travellers neared the rest house, four guards standing outside the guest house approached them with their swords unsheathed. 'Stop!' they ordered. Another guard who was standing at the entrance of the rest house was holding a brightly burning torch. The swords held by the guards glowed in the torchlight.

When the warrior mounted on the horse showed them the insignia, they respectfully made way for him and approached Paranjyothi. The warrior mounted on the horse turned around and announced, 'He has come with me!' They made way for Paranjyothi too.

The elder traveller showed the aforesaid insignia to the overseer of the rest house and instructed, 'Both of us need to stay at the rest house tonight. Our horses need to be fed.'

The head of the rest house, like the other guards, respectfully responded, 'As you say, aiyya.' Paranjyothi, who observed all this, was surprised. He surmised that the elder traveller was on an important state mission. He wondered if the elder traveller was a powerful commander in the Pallava army. Once the task on hand was complete, Paranjyothi wanted to find his co-traveller again in order to befriend him.

When both of them were partaking their dinner, the warrior told Paranjyothi, 'Thambi, didn't I talk about the Vyjayanthi war? During those times, I was more or less of your age. I stayed at this guesthouse then. One night, I had a strange experience!'

'What was that?' asked Paranjyothi eagerly.

'Thambi, we have been conversing thus far without knowing each other's name. I have no objection to introducing myself. My parents named me Vajrabahu. But my friends call me Kumbakarnan. I am a sound sleeper. Once, like today, after having travelled the whole day, I was in deep slumber. Do you know what happened then?'

'You must have woken up screaming after dreaming of ghosts!' quipped Paranjyothi mischievously.

Hearing this, Vajrabahu laughed and said, 'Oh no! Something more dangerous than that happened! I dreamt that the house had collapsed on me and opened my eyes. Five to six ruffians were sitting on me. Two of them were searching my waist. Do you know why?'

'Aiyya! Do you think I am a clairvoyant? If you don't tell me, how will I know?' asked Paranjyothi.

'Well, thambi, they wanted to misappropriate the message I was carrying for Commander Kalipahayar. Those ruffians thought that I would have fastened the missive to my waist.'

'Ah!' said Paranjyothi. Unconsciously, his hand went to the right side of his waist. It lasted only for a second. The next moment his hand returned to its original position.

But that slight action did not escape the warrior Vajrabahu's hawk-like eyes.

'Then what happened, aiyya? Did the ruffians find the message you were carrying?' asked Paranjyothi.

'They did not get the epistle. They got seven to eight knocks on their heads with my knuckles! After receiving the knocks, they fled, thankful that their heads were still intact!'

Paranjyothi laughingly said, 'Those fools deserved that! Didn't they disturb your deep slumber? Had one man come alone and felt your waist, he would have probably found the missive.'

'Even then he would not have found it,' said Vajrabahu.

'Why not? Didn't you mention that you sleep like Kumbakarnan?'

'That's true, thambi! But only if the message had been fastened to my waist would he have found it.'

'Then in which safe place did you keep it?'

'I handed it over to Agni Bhagavan.'

'What is this? Aren't you a conscientious messenger? Why did you travel after burning the epistle?'

'Before burning the missive, I read it carefully and committed it to memory.'

'Oh! Are royal emissaries permitted to act in this manner?'

'A man who is incapable of quick thinking and appropriate action is unfit to be a royal emissary. Thambi, I anticipated the occurrence of such danger. So, I acted with caution. For this, I also received an award from the chakravarthy.'

Hearing all this, Paranjyothi was confused. He remembered the bikshu cautioning him not to sleep in the same room as others, should he happen to spend the night at a rest house.

Fortunately, he was provided with a separate room that night. Vajrabahu took leave of him and asked him to go to bed saying, 'Thambi, from now, our ways part. I will leave early tomorrow morning. I like you very much. Don't hesitate to approach me if you are in need of assistance.'

***

Since Paranjyothi remembered the incidents Vajrabahu had related as he was going to bed, he was determined not to sleep soundly and to wake up promptly should there be noise. But his age and the fatigue from having travelled all day caused him to sleep as soon as he lay down.

He was unable to sleep peacefully, though. He was subjected to one nightmare after another. He dreamt that he too had turned into a ghost and was wandering ceaselessly in the midst of phantom horsemen, in an area filled with crimson purasa flowers. After roaming around a lot, he was tired and lay down in a mountain cave. He dreamt that he was sleeping! But he was conscious even while sleeping. Only his eyes were closed. One ghost after another came and felt his waist. He thought, 'Fortunately, the message is not fastened to my waist. I have placed it beneath my head.' He believed that if he were to open his eyes, the ghosts would run away. But he was unable to open his eyes despite much effort.

Then, at a distance, a fire-spewing ghost appeared. Along with it, a black ghost approached him. Both came closer and closer to him! The light from the fire emanating from the ghost's mouth hurt his closed eyes. Finally, unable to withstand the heat, his eyelids opened.

But those who approached him were neither the fire-spewing ghost nor the black ghost. It was the warrior Vajrabahu followed by the rest house's overseer carrying a lantern.

Paranjyothi woke up with a start. His right hand reached out for the spear that lay next to him.

33

Theft of Message

Vajrabahu remarked in a relaxed tone, 'Patience, thambi! Instead of grabbing the spear, practise restraint. We are not phantoms or ghosts. You teased me asking if I dreamt of ghosts. Everyone in this rest house woke up hearing you scream as though you had seen ghosts.'

When Paranjyothi recollected that he had indeed dreamt of ghosts, he smiled in embarrassment. He then asked, 'Is it dawn? May we leave?'

'It is midnight now. Even when you were lying down securely in the rest house you were blabbering out fearfully. How will you travel by yourself in the middle of the night? You were screaming, "Amma! Amma!" in your sleep. If you do intend travelling by yourself now, please let us know the whereabouts of that pious soul! We will at least let her know of your fate,' said Vajrabahu.

These words pricked Paranjyothi's heart like sharp thorns.

'Didn't you relate such frightful tales last night? That's why I had nightmares,' replied Paranjyothi in a conciliatory tone.

'That's all right! Try to sleep peacefully for some time. I will leave this lamp here,' said the warrior Vajrabahu.

Leaving the lamp there, Vajrabahu and the head of the rest house left Paranjyothi's room.

* * *

After they had left, Paranjyothi tried to close his eyes and sleep, but he was unable to. He tossed and turned. He sat up and then lay down again. Sleep still evaded him. The lamp which they had left on one side pricked his eyes. For a moment, he thought of extinguishing the light. Then he remembered something vividly. He picked up the slim bamboo tube that was wrapped in cloth and kept by his head. He took out the bunch of palm leaf manuscripts from inside the tube and sat beside the lamp.

He opened the missive and looked at them intently. Ah! How disappointing! Something was written on the palm leaves, but what was it? He was unable to decipher it. The message was not in Tamil. It was in Sanskrit, Prakrit or Pali. Ah! How essential education was! It did not suffice if one knew just one's mother tongue. One must know the other languages spoken in a nation. Paranjyothi now regretted wasting his time without educating himself and not even learning Tamil thoroughly.

After all these days, he had come to Kanchi for an education. Did that happen? Did all the commotion about war have to coincide with his arrival? Did this dangerous task have to land on his head? As Paranjyothi was thinking thus, he felt sleepy. His eyelids felt heavy and his eyes closed involuntarily. Deep sleep overpowered him. He lost all consciousness in some time. The palm leaves slipped from his hand and lay scattered on the floor.

***

After some time, the door of Paranjyothi's room opened gently. Vajrabahu silently came in. He collected the manuscripts that lay on the floor, closed the door, and left.

Vajrabahu then entered a large corner room that was two or three rooms away from Paranjyothi's. He sat by an illuminated metal lamp and attentively read the missive he had appropriated from Paranjyothi.

For some time, he intently looked at the epistle. His eyebrows were knotted and his forehead was creased. Now and then he looked up at the roof in deep thought. Sometimes he clenched his fists, looked down and laughed. He then stared at the lamp intently. Finally, his face glowed. He then read the messages inscribed on the four leaves quickly and enthusiastically.

He then took four blank palm leaves that lay next to him, cut them to the same size as the original, and began writing. He quickly completed writing something and compared what he had written with Paranjyothi's missive. He carefully kept the original away and walked towards Paranjyothi's room with the missive he had written. He saw Paranjyothi still lying unconscious beside the lamp, which was now about to be extinguished. The room was filled with smoke that emitted a strange odour. Vajrabahu covered his nose and mouth and entered the room. He left the new missive in the same place as the original, pulled the lamp's wick inwards, dipped it in oil and extinguished the lamp. He did all this very swiftly and left the room the very next moment.

When Vajrabahu returned to his room, he carefully read the messgage Paranjyothi had brought. He then burnt the palm leaves one by one in the flame of the lamp. As he was engaged in this act, his face revealed that he was deep in thought.

After burning the four palm leaves to ashes, he resumed writing on another four palm leaves. He did not write quickly and continuously, like before. He stopped from time to time, thought for a while, and then wrote. When he was done and had placed the palm leaves in a tube, the eastern horizon glowed. Towards the west, the half-moon lost its brilliance and assumed a dim hue. The glow from the stars was diminishing. Birds chirped sporadically.

***

When Paranjyothi woke up, the tender rays of the rising sun were streaming into the room through the balcony. He immediately collected the palm leaves that lay scattered on the floor, put them in the tube, and fastened it around his waist. He recollected having nightmares the previous night. He also remembered Vajrabahu and the rest house head leaving the lamp for him, his attempt at reading the missive, and finally falling asleep. He still felt slightly dizzy. His stomach felt vaguely uncomfortable.

He noticed that there was a strange odour in the room. But all this did not hold his attention for long. The shame on account of having slept after leaving the manuscript on the floor superseded all other thoughts. When he heard the sound of horse hooves, he rushed to the entrance. He observed that the head of the rest house and guards were looking at a horse that was speeding away in the distance.

When he exclaimed, 'Oh! Is Vajrabahu leaving? Has he left so early?' they turned around and looked at him.

When the horse had disappeared from their sight, Paranjyothi asked the guards, 'Aiyya! Who is Vajrabahu? Do you know?'

One of the guards responded, 'We thought you would inform us of his identity!'

'Were you so respectful to him yesterday without knowing who he was?'

'We were deferential not without a reason. Do you know he carried an insignia with the lion symbol?'

'What is so special about the lion insignia?'

'Only those travelling on extremely important government missions carry the lion insignia!'

One of the guards asked the other, 'Who could he have been?'

'He may be one of the ministers,' said a guard.

'I heard that the chakravarthy is about to dismiss Commander Kalipahayar and appoint a new commander. It could be the new commander,' said another guard.

'Do you know the reason for changing the commander?' asked the overseer.

'What else could be the reason? It seems that the Vatapi army is approaching north Pennai. Isn't the fact that the commander is still retaining the army at the northern provinces reason enough?'

'It seems Commander Kalipahayar has gone to Kanchi to seek the chakravarthy's counsel. Is that why the chakravarthy was angry? He apparently said, "Enough of you occupying the commander's post!"'

Paranjyothi, who was listening to this conversation, said, 'Aiyya, where is my horse? I need to leave.'

After asking Paranjyothi some questions about himself, the guards said, 'Where are you headed to?'

Paranjyothi responded, 'I need to go to the Buddhist monastery on the banks of north Pennai. How far is it from here?'

They pointed to the direction in which Vajrabahu had left and said, 'If you take this route, you will reach north Pennai by noon. From there, head west along the river bank. The Buddhist monastery is at the confluence of the Papagni and North Pennai rivers.'

They lead Paranjyothi's horse to him. As Paranjyothi mounted the horse, he thought, 'Ah! Vajrabahu also went in this direction. I should have woken up earlier and left with him. Had I done so, the journey would have been so interesting. I could have happily listened to his stories and felt no fatigue.'

34

Monastery

The evening of memorable adventures for Paranjyothi coincided with him being discussed in Kanchi. The heir to the Pallava dynasty, Kumara Chakravarthy Mamalla Narasimhar, and the heir to the Saivite bhakti movement, Thirunavukkarasar Swamigal, were engaged in conversation.

***

After returning from Mamallapuram, Mahendra chakravarthy, along with his dear son, had ventured out of the fort incognito. In the dim starlit night, they left their horses in a secluded place and walked along the ramparts that ran adjacent to the moat.

When the sound of a boat sailing in the moat was heard, Narasimhar was taken aback. Mahendrar gestured for him to keep quiet. Both of them hid behind the nearby bushes.

Yes, a boat was indeed sailing in the moat. The boatman was exercising extreme caution in wielding the oars so that he would make no noise. The boat reached the bank that was near the ramparts. Two people alighted from the boat. Both of them pulled the boat to the banks. They hid the boat in a dense bush that grew by the ramparts.

They went and stood near the ramparts. The very next moment, they mysteriously disappeared! Just like a gigantic spider which remained calm immediately after swallowing a couple of mosquitoes, the Kanchi fort also returned to tranquility after consuming the two men in the bat of an eyelid.

Before the kumara chakravarthy could recover from the shock of witnessing these events, another astonishing incident occurred. From a nearby bush, another man suddenly emerged. After prostrating before the chakravarthy, he stood deferentially.

Seeing him, Mahendrar, who did not display an iota of surprise, asked, 'Shatrugna, can you guess where the door in the rampart leads to?'

'It probably leads to the rear of the Buddha statue at the royal viharam, swami,' said Shatrugnan.

'The man who constructed the door in the ramparts must be extremely skilful, isn't he?'

'The man who painted the door must be more skilful than the one who built it, my lord! In my anxiety, I examined all these places. The existence of a door was not apparent.'

'Very good. Shatrugna, I am travelling to the north tomorrow.'

'I am prepared too, prabhu.'

'No, you don't have to accompany me. Shadow Naganandi till I assign you to another mission . . .'

'If he were to leave Thondai Nadu . . .'

'Even then.'

'If he were to go to Chola Nadu or Pandya Nadu . . .'

'You must follow him. If he were to send a written message through someone . . . ?'

'I know what to do, swami. But, what about the epistle he has sent with the youth from Sengattankudi . . . ?'

'I will take care of that. Under no circumstance should you lose sight of Naganandi. All important news should be communicated to me.'

'As you command, prabhu!'

***

When the chakravarthy and Mamallar returned to the palace, Mamallar asked, 'Shouldn't we immediately shut down the royal viharam and seal the entrance at the fort wall?'

'Not now, my child. We will do it at the appropriate time. For the time being, movements at that entrance will help us understand our foes' treacheries,' responded the chakravarthy.

***

After the chakravarthy headed northwards, Mamallar found it very difficult to spend time within the Kanchi fort. Observing the chakravarthy deduce that it was the bikshu and Paranjyothi hiding behind the Buddha statue at Aayanar's residence, and locating the secret entrance to the fort, Mamallar's respect for him had increased multifold. Hence, he did not even think of going against his father's command prohibiting him from leaving the Kanchi fort.

However, he was troubled at the thought of being idly confined within the fort when there were momentous occurrences in the kingdom and a major war was imminent.

The Pallava forces were being mobilized in Kazhukunram. Mamallar regretted that he had not secured his father's permission to at least go there and oversee the army. If only he had obtained his father's permission to proceed further to Mamallapuram!

Yes, Mamallar remembered Sivakami often even while thinking of several other issues. Had she seen the spear he had drawn between the lotus and fawn she sketched? Would she have understood the message? Would the message have satisfied her?

She was unaware of the promise he had made to his father, so she would be angry that he did not visit her. Why couldn't she come here? But how could she come here? His father had issued such a categorical command to Aayanar. How could he leave his work and come here?

The kumara chakravarthy was immersed in several such thoughts. As he was idle, he felt even sadder.

***

Mamallar thought of securing an audience with Thirunavukkarasar Swamigal when the latter returned to Kanchi. The chakravarthy had asked him to communicate a message to the swamigal. So, one day he visited Navukkarasar's monastery, which was close the Ekambareshwarar temple.

Navukkarasar affectionately welcomed the kumara chakravarthy and described the greatness of the temples he had visited. He enquired about the chakravarthy's journey to the north and the impending war.

Then the swamigal said, 'Mamallar! I thought of conveying a message to the chakravarthy. As he is not here, I am telling you. I am desirous of relocating our monastery from here to Thirumetralli. As the monastery is located in the heart of the city, there is no peace. Also, there are constant arguments between my disciples and students of northern languages in the nearby school. Despite explaining several times that it was Lord Shiva who bestowed both Aryam and Tamil on this earth, they do not understand. Aren't they still in their youth? So they are bound to be aggressive. We are unable to tolerate the troubles caused by the kabalikas at the Ekambareshwarar temple. So, I am thinking of seeking refuge in God at Thirumetralli. It is more peaceful than this place.'

Mamallar, who had been listening devotedly, said, 'Swami. I had suggested previously that we ought to chase away the kabalikas from the Ekambareshwarar temple. You had refused. There is no objection to your establishing the monastery at Thirumetralli. But let me tell you what the chakravarthy had asked me convey to you. Then you may act as you deem fit. The Pallavendra says that war may occur in Thondai Mandalam, and Kanchi may be subject to a siege. He opines that it would be good if you could go on a pilgrimage to Chola Nadu and Pandya Nadu till the war is over. The chakravarthy also feels it would be good if the monastery is closed during this time. Please consider this and decide as you wish.'

Navukkarasar thought for some time and said, 'I agree with the chakravarthy's suggestion. But I wish I had known this earlier. I had sent for Aayanar. I intended to ask him to start building ill monastery at Thirumetralli . . . That is also for the good. Before embarking on a long journey, I can meet the respected sculptor.'

Mamallar felt joyous when he heard that Aayanar was coming. He eagerly asked, 'When is Aayanar coming, swami?'

When Navukkarasar Peruman said, 'He may come this evening itself,' Mamallar decided to stay at the monastery till Aayanar arrived.

'Swami, do you know that Aayanar has sent the youth from Thirusengattankudi who came bearing a message for you to Nagarjuna mountain?' he asked.

When the swamigal said, 'What is that? I don't know anything,' Narasimhar told him everything he knew about Paranjyothi.

As they were conversing, a disciple rushed inside announcing, 'Aayanar is coming!' Everyone's eyes turned towards the entrance.

35

Second Arangetram

During the time in which this story is set, Thirunavukkarasar must have been about fifty-five years old. That revered soul's golden-hued body was smeared with pure white vibhuti. Strings of rudraksha beads adorned his neck and chest. Rudraksha beads were fastened around his forehead and wrists. He had wrapped a pure white cloth around his waist. His face glowed with wisdom. The divine grace in Navukkarasar's eyes was a reflection of his spiritual thinking and the frequent shedding of tears of devotion. The imprint of the hoe with which he mowed the grass at the temple praharam could be seen on his shoulders.

Though Thirunavukkarasar headed the monastery he had established at Kanchi, he used to go on pilgrimage periodically. He visited several Shiva temples in Thondai Nadu and Chola Nadu and sang hymns that were steeped in devotion and showcased the richness of Tamil. Wherever he went, people accorded him a rousing welcome, seated him in a palanquin and took him in procession.He himself cut the grass growing at the praharams of he temples he visited with his hoe. Thousands of people witnessed the service to Lord Shiva in amazement. They then decided to keep their temples clean.

People were keen that Thirunavukkarasar should sing hymns in praise of the temples in their vicinity. Many requested him, 'You must visit our village too. You must sing hymns glorifying our temple.'

The hymns the great soul sang in this fashion at many places were written down on palm leaf manuscripts. People were ecstatic recollecting the honour bestowed on them. Wherever the great Navukkarasar went, people flocked to see the divine aura his face exuded, and waited eagerly to listen to his nectar-like discourses.

Today, when Navukkarasar's disciple announced Aayanar's arrival at his monastery, everyone turned in unison towards the entrance, a manifestation of the high esteem everyone held Aayanar in.

The kumara chakravarthy, who was seated next to Navukkarasar was the most restless amongst those assembled. The possibility of Sivakami accompanying Aayanar made him very happy. The very next moment it occurred to Mamallar that Sivakami may not have come; this dampened his enthusiasm. His alternating feelings of happiness and dejection did not last too long. Aayanar reached the entrance. Ah! What was that *jal jal* sound? It sounded like anklets! There was no doubt that the girl following Aayanar was Sivakami!

The kumara chakravarthy's eyes sought out Sivakami. Sivakami's eyes eagerly met his. Sivakami's crestfallen face bloomed for a moment. But only for a moment! The next second, her lotus-like face was all fire and brimstone. Sivakami followed her father into that hall with her face lowered.

The exchange of glances went unnoticed in the joyous tumult around.

Thirunavukkarasar, who was known for his humility, stood up from his seat and walked four steps forward saying, 'Welcome, the emperor of sculpture!'

Aayanar, hearing this, hastened forward saying, 'How sacrilegious!' and prostrated before him.

When Navukkarasar got up from his seat, his disciples had followed suit. After Navukkarasar and Aayanar sat down, they too took their appointed places.

Even after everyone had sat down, Sivakami continued standing behind her father with her head bowed. That's when Navukkarasar saw her and asked, 'Ah! Who is this girl, Aayanar? Is she your daughter, Sivakami?'

Aayanar said, 'Yes, adigal. When I said that I am coming here for an audience with you, she said that she would join me. I brought her along.'

'I am very happy. I was keen to meet your daughter. I have heard of the unparalleled proficiency she has attained in dancing. Didn't her arangetram happen recently? I was not there then,' remarked Navukkarasar.

'I regretted your absence, swami. That day, when Rudrachariar saw her dance, he was stunned. It was then that he acknowledged that dance formed the basis of sculpture, painting and music. He openly stated in the court that it was only after seeing Sivakami's dance that he realized that he had a lot more to learn in music.'

As Aayanar was speaking thus, his face and voice brimmed with pride. Then Thirunavukkarasar, who was also known as Vageechar, smilingly said, 'Aayanar, even the divine process of creation, preservation and destruction is based on dance! Isn't Lord Shiva, who is the Creator, the Guardian and the Destroyer of this world, found dancing at Chidambaram?'

The kumara chakravarthy, who had been silent thus far, said, 'Swami, Aayanar's daughter performed abhinayams to one of your hymns that describes Lord Nataraja's ananda natanam. Your Holiness should definitely watch that piece!'

'Yes, swami. Sivakami was supposed to perform to three of your hymns, but she was able to perform to only one of them. You must have heard of the news that interrupted the arangetram.' When Aayanar said this, it seemed that he had not gotten over the sorrow the event had caused.

'I heard about it, Aayanar. It wasn't just Sivakami's arangetram that was disrupted because of the war. Several other tasks seem to have been affected. Even the assignment I called you for falls in this category!' said Vageecha Peruman.

'Swami, for what job did you call me?' asked Aayanar.

'I was desirous of relocating this monastery from Ekambareshwarar's sannadhi* to Thirumettrali. As this place is located in the heart of the city, it is not appropriate for education. Thirumettrali is the abode of peace. In the garden surrounding the temple, jasmine and golden laburnum are in full bloom. There is no commotion in the streets. Thirumettrali is the appropriate place to contemplate the divine and to learn Tamil.'

When Aayanar said, 'Perumane, are you going to compose a hymn dedicated to the reigning deity of Thirumettrali?' Navukkarasar looked towards his disciples.

* Lord Ekambareshwarar's sanctum. Refers to Kanchi.

Immediately, a disciple sang the following lines from the Thirumettrali pathigam:

Having Parvati as half His body
Glorified by a son like Murugan
Covered by fragrant jasmine garlands
Adorned by the golden-hued laburnum
Like the fire within the sun
He graces Kanchi His abode,
The seat of learning.

When the disciple rendered the song in his soulful voice, Navukkarasar's eyes were filled with tears. He was ecstatic when he had a vision of Lord Shiva glowing like the sun, adorned with jasmine and golden laburnum from the Thirumettrali temple. Seeing this, the others present in the hall became ecstatic.

For some time after the rendition of the song was over, silence prevailed. Then Navukkarasar came out of his euphoric state and looked at those around him. Immediately, Aayanar said, 'Adigal, you are truly the king of the spoken word! Your hymns are soul-stirring. As Kanchi and Thirumettrali find place in your hymn, they will attain immortality. I am ready to begin constructing the Thirumettrali monastery, as per your wishes. But the chakravarthy has commanded me to hasten the completion of an important assignment at the harbour city. The kumara chakravarthy should command which task needs to be completed first.' So saying, Aayanar looked towards Mamallar.

Before Mamallar could respond to Aayanar's query, Navukkarasar said: 'There's no need for that, respected sculptor. As you were entering, Mamallar was conveying the chakravarthy's opinion to me. The chakravarthy feels that, till the war is over, I should go on a pilgrimage to the holy cities in Chola Nadu and Pandya Nadu, accompanied by my disciples. I too have harboured this desire for a long time. The Kanchi fort may become the target of our foes' siege. During such times, it is better for monks like us to be uninvolved.'

After listening to Navukkarasar, Narasimha Varmar said, 'Adigal, your view is laudable. Wouldn't it be good if Jain monks and bikshus concurred with your view and did not interfere with matters of the state?'

Aayanar felt a prick when he heard the word bikshu. He was also reminded of Paranjyothi. 'Adigal, I forgot to tell you something. A boy from Thirusengattankudi in Chola Nadu had come to enroll in your monastery and learn Tamil. He carried messages for you and me from Thiruvengadu Namasivaya Vaidyar. I have sent him to Sri Parvatham in the north to learn a critical secret related to the art of painting . . .'

'Did you send him so far? Isn't it a war zone? Didn't you say that he was a young boy?' asked a slightly worried Navukkarasar.

'Though is young, he is extremely brave, swami!' So saying, he related the incident of Paranjyothi flinging the spear at the mad elephant on the day of the arangetram.

Finally Aayanar said, 'I will send Paranjyothi to you as soon as he returns, swami!'

'No need, Aayanar. I do not know where I will be when he returns. Since he is of service to you, let him be your disciple. One does not get the opportunity to learn the art of sculpture easily. Can there be an art more superior to sculpting indestructible temples for the eternal God . . . ?'

Aayanar interjected saying, 'Adigal, there is an art that is superior to sculpture. Our stone temples may be ruined beyond recognition. But then your temple of poetry cannot be destroyed. Your poetry has an everlasting place in the future.'

Then the kumara chakravarthy said, 'Have you both forgotten what you agreed upon some time ago? Isn't dance the foundation of all the arts?' Hearing this, everyone present smiled. But Sivakami alone continued standing with her head bowed.

Navukkarasar said, 'True, kumara chakravarthy. We did forget. Dance is the basis of all the arts. While in the presence of the Peruman at Thillai, one becomes ecstatic and poetry gushes forth like a flood; the same does not happen in the presence of other deities.' He then turned to Aayanar and said, 'Respected sculptor, shouldn't I witness your daughter dancing? I do not know when I will return from my pilgrimage to the south. I do not wish to leave without seeing the renowned Sivakami dance. It would suffice if she performed abhinayams for just one song!'

Aayanar said, 'Swami, Sivakami is fortunate to perform in your presence.' He then turned around and looked at Sivakami. Seeing her standing with her head bowed without a trace of happiness, Aayanar was surprised.

Observing this, Mamallar told Navukkarasar, 'Probably Sivakami does not want to dance since I am here. Swami, let me take leave of you.'

Hearing this, Sivakami looked up with a start and asked, 'Appa, to which song should I perform abhinayams?' as she stood ready to dance. Her beauty was comparable to that of a fawn and her voice to that of a cuckoo when she asked this.

'Why don't you first perform to *Poovanathu Punithanar*?' asked Aayanar happily. Sivakami's second arangetram commenced in the presence of Navukkarasar*, Kalai Arasar† and Illavarasar‡. Sivakami sang the following verse in a sonorous voice, while simultaneously performing the appropriate gestures and abhinayams. The *jal, jal* sound from her anklets resonated rhythmically to the song and to the refrain 'appears', as well.

The perfect trident glitteringly appears
The crescent on matted hair glowingly appears
The fragrant konrai teasingly appears
The conch earrings brilliantly appear
The blanket of elephant skin ragingly appears
The enticing hair dancingly appears
The smeared ash charmingly appears
Now . . . lo behold our Lord!
In the bewitching gardens of Thiruppuvanam

When Sivakami sang this divine song and performed abhinayams according to its meaning, everyone was mesmerized. They lost all consciousness of time and place.

When Navukkarasar's disciple had sung some time ago, the honey-like Tamil words had resonated in the listeners' ears. Their eyes sought out Navukkarasar. Their hearts melted at the sight of Navukkarasar becoming rapturous while listening to the song.

When Sivakami performed abhinayams, the audience did not look at Navukkarasar. Neither the kumara chakravarthy nor Aayanar were visible to them. Their eyes did not see

---

* King of the spoken word. 'Navu', in Tamil, means 'tongue'.
† King of arts; refers to Aayanar.
‡ Crown prince; refers to Mamallar.

the walls and pillars of the monastery, nor the paintings and sculptures on the walls.

They did not even see Sivakami, who was singing and dancing in front of them!

They saw Lord Shiva himself appear before them!

They saw the trident in his hands and the crescent moon on his matted locks.

They saw the garland around his neck and the white conches that adorned his ears.

They saw his body covered with vibhuti.

They lost all consciousness while witnessing this divine sight. They forgot the earth and were transported to Kailasam.

Only sometime after the singing and abhinayams had ceased did they regain their consciousness and return to earth.

When everyone had regained their consciousness, their attention turned to Navukkarasar. They witnessed tears flowing down like streams and moistening his vibhuti-smeared body.

Several amongst them wondered if the great soul sitting in front of them was indeed Lord Shiva whom they had witnessed for so long in their mind's eye.

After some time, Navukkarasar said in a faltering tone, 'Aayanar! Your daughter made Lord Shiva who resides in Kailasam appear in front of us!'

Aayanar, his eyes brimming with tears of joy, said, 'It's all due to your blessings, swami!' He then looked at Sivakami and said, 'Will you perform abhinayams for another song, my dear? Let it be a song from Agathurai!'

36

Vageechar's Blessing

When Aayanar asked Sivakami to perform to a song from Agathurai, she sang a verse from Navukkarasar's Thiruvarur Thandagam, set to the *Pazham Pancharam* ragam.

A maiden is moved listening to the divine name of the Lord for the first time. Her devotion gradually transforms into love, which intensifies and engulfs her heart. The devotional hymn that relates this story is as follows:

At first His name she heard
About His image then she heard
Later of His abode Aaroor she heard
Besotted with love she lost her self
From parents and the rest
She estranged herself
Gave up all tradition and upbringing
Sublimated her name and self
Steadfast in her resolve

To meditate lifelong
At the feet of our Lord

At first, Sivakami sang just the verse. After that, she sang as she performed abhinayams. Those watching her felt she was love personified. The audience saw the bashful happiness of a woman in love for the first time. They saw the joy she felt, during the initial days, on hearing the lover's name and other personal details. On listening to others describing his exploits, the subtle changes wrought in her bearing unfolded before them. The viewers saw how mesmerized a woman was as her love intensified and the extent of the sacrifice she was willing to make for her love and lover; she was emboldened to leave her parents, to flout social norms and ignore societal disapproval.

When Sivakami portrayed the above emotions that were beyond description, the viewers thought, 'This is not the love ordinary humans experience. It is the love one has for the God of the Universe, Lord Shiva!'

Sivakami did not stop at this. For love to be fulfilled, one had to go a step further. Even though a woman is ready to make great sacrifices for her lover, he is not satisfied. To test her love further, one day her lover suddenly disappears. The woman, who is indescribably sad, forgets the world around her. She forgets herself too. She even forgets her name. When someone asks, 'What is your name?' she states her lover's name! In this state of mind, when her lover returns, she prostrates before him, apologizing and asking forgiveness for mistakes she has not committed.

Sivakami progressively portrayed these emotions through her expressions, eyes and movements. She finally sang

Steadfast in her resolve

To meditate lifelong
At the feet of our Lord

She brought both her hands together to form a namaskaram and finally dropped to the floor like a felled tree.

Everyone who had assembled appreciatively exclaimed, 'Ha! Ha! Ha!' Aayanar stood up calling out, 'Sivakami!' He rushed towards his daughter. An agitated Mamallar followed him.

Aayanar sat on the floor next to Sivakami. He was shivering. Seeing this, Mamallar gently lifted Sivakami's head and placed it on Aayanar's lap, the way a devotee would collect tender flowers to offer God.

Those present in the hall rushed towards the trio and surrounded them. Some of them said, 'Bring a fan!' while others called for water.

Someone said, 'Please make way!' Navukkarasar Peruman stood up from his seat and walked towards Sivakami. He shot a sympathetic glance at Sivakami, who lay unconscious on Aayanar's lap. He applied vibhuti on Sivakami's forehead.

For a while there was pin-drop silence.

Sivakami's eyes slowly opened, like a dark kuvalai flower blooming at dawn.

When she opened her eyes, she first saw Navukkarasar. As she lay on her father's lap, she brought both her hands together and performed a namaskaram to that great soul.

Vageechar blessed her saying, 'May you lead a blessed and prosperous life, my child!'

Hearing his benediction, a slight smile appeared on Sivakami's ruby lips that looked like a red water-lily shyly and hesitantly unfolding in a lake filled with lotuses.

Then her black eyes moved in all directions, as though they were looking for something. They finally rested on the kumara chakravarthy's face.

Her eyes seemed to say, 'Did you hear how the adigal blessed me?' and also communicated her intention to forgive him for his faults and befriend him again.

When she heard Navukkarasar's voice again, Sivakami regained her consciousness completely and sat up with a start. She felt embarrassed that she had fainted in front of so many people.

Vageechar said, 'I have read and heard about the greatness of Bharatanatyam. But only today did I realize its distinction entirely. Before today, I never realized that my hymns were capable of arousing such emotion. Your daughter will bring greater glory to the Bharata Shastram. It will truly become a divine art. It is a wonderful art that is to be dedicated to the Lord who dances at Thillai . . .'

As the Swami uttered these encouraging words, they heard the sound of a horse rapidly approaching them. That horse stopped at the entrance to the monastery. Immediately, the kumara chakravarthy walked towards the entrance.

Mamallar briefly spoke to the guard standing there and returned inside. He approached Navukkarasar with folded palms and said, 'Swami, emissaries from Madurai have arrived bearing some urgent news. I will take leave of you.'

'Certainly, kumara chakravarthy. When you're sending a message to your father, please let him know that I will embark on a pilgrimage to the south in deference to his wishes.'

'So be it, swami.' Mamallar then turned to Aayanar and said, 'Respected sculptor! When you reach the harbour, please let me know of Sivakami's well-being. For certain reasons, I cannot leave Kanchi for some time.'

As he was speaking thus, Mamallar was desirous of taking leave of Sivakami through eye contact. But Sivakami was standing behind Aayanar with her head bowed.

So, Mamallar had to go without taking leave of Sivakami. He left in a rush, mindless of Navukkarasar Peruman's presence. His anger was evident.

Within a few minutes, the sound of a horse-drawn chariot was heard outside.

Sivakami felt as though her soul had left her without even informing her and had mounted the chariot.

When it was time for Aayanar and Sivakami to take leave, Navukkarasar gestured to Aayanar to stay back. He spoke in a soft tone so that Sivakami could not hear

'Aayanar! Your daughter has been blessed with a wonderful art, a divine art. That is why I am concerned about her. When God endows such great talent on someone, he also subjects them to harsh trials. You know how many tribulations he put me through before accepting me . . .'

On hearing these words, Aayanar, who had been extremely happy till some time ago, became agitated and asked, 'Swami! What are you saying? You cannot compare a great soul like yourself with a naïve girl like Sivakami! Why should she be subject to trials? I am concerned that a holy person like you should utter these words!'

'Aayanar, don't speak loudly! There is no need for Sivakami to know. But please be cautious. On seeing your daughter, I realized that extreme sorrow lies in store for her. Ah! Why did God bestow me with this foresight!' As Navukkarasar was speaking, his eyes brimmed with tears. 'But you must be courageous. It is our duty to serve this world. It is the duty of God, who is the embodiment of mercy, to protect us. You should carry out your duties calmly.

You should not lose resolve when you face hardship. When God subjects his dear ones to harsh trials, he ultimately blesses them.'

After saying this, Navukkarasar Peruman went back into the monastery. Aayanar, who had come to the monastery joyously, left with a heavy heart. It seemed as though a massive boulder, like the ones from which he created exquisite sculptures, had been placed on his chest.

37

Kannabiran

Aayanar left the monastery with a heavy heart after hearing Navukkarasar's prediction. Controlling his emotions, he asked Sivakami, 'My child! Shall we return home?'

Sivakami responded, 'Appa, let's visit Kamali and return tomorrow morning.' Even as she was talking, a chariot drawn by two horses came to a halt in front of them. The chariot driver jumped down from his seat and approached Aayanar and Sivakami. He was well-built and was about twenty-five years old.

'Aiyya! Apparently the sculptor Aayanar and his daughter Sivakami have come here. Have you seen them?' he enquired.

'Oh! Is that Kannabiran? Are you unable to recognize us?' asked Aayanar.

'Am I able to recognize you? I have seen this flat nose and broad ears somewhere, I cannot recollect,' said Kannabiran knocking his own head.

'Appane, don't break your head and blame us! Then Kamali will not spare us. We are the sculptor Aayanar and Sivakami whom you came looking for,' said Aayanar.

'Why didn't you tell me this earlier? I was doubtful too. But I acted in accordance with what Jambavan had told Kumbakarnan: "What you observe is not the truth! What you hear is not the truth! The truth is understood only after thorough enquiry." But who amongst the two of you is the sculptor Aayanar and who is Sivakami?' asked the chariot driver, who was also a jester. He looked at their faces intently in the dim twilight.

Sivakami burst out laughing and then said, 'Anna! I am Sivakami and this is my father. We are standing on planet earth and the sky is above us. Your name is Kannabiran and my sister's name is Kamali. Now do you recollect everything? How is akka? We were thinking of visiting your home tonight.'

'Oh! Is that so? It seems like the God whom we had intended visiting at the temple has come of his own accord to meet us! Were you planning to visit our home?'

'Yes. May we come or not?'

'On the one hand, you may come. On the other, you may not.'

'Appa, let us return to our house. Please come!' said Sivakami in an angry tone.

'Please don't say that! You must definitely come. Do you know what Kamali told me as I was leaving home today? "It seems that the sculptor Aayanar is coming to Navukkarasar's monastery today. My friend Sivakami may accompany him. You must bring them both home tonight." I replied, "They belong to high society, Kamali! Will they come to the residence of poor people like us? Even if they come, will they stay?" Kamali shot back, "Tell them that I am on my death bed!"'

'Oh! Is Kamali not keeping good health?' enquired a concerned Aayanar.

'Yes, aiyya! Kamali's life is gradually leaving her as she has not seen her friend for the last one year. Three-fourths of her soul has already left her. It would be good if you could come before the remaining soul departs.'

'In that case, let's go immediately. People have congregated here,' said Sivakami.

Truly, there was a crowd around them. It was not surprising that the sight of Aayanar and Sivakami conversing with the palace charioteer in that busy thoroughfare had attracted people's attention.

Sivakami and Aayanar mounted the chariot Kannabiran had brought along. That beautiful royal chariot drawn by two horses and driven by the foremost charioteer of the Pallava kingdom made its way through the wide streets of Kanchi.

As they were traveling in the chariot, Sivakami asked, 'Anna! You said that "on the other hand, you should not come". Why is that?'

'Thangachi, didn't I fetch the kumara chakravarthy from the monastery? As soon as he alighted at the palace entrance, he said, "Kanna! Take the chariot to the monastery. Collect Aayanar and his daughter from the monastery and leave them at Mamallapuram. Don't listen to them even if they refuse!" After the kumara chakravarthy has commanded thus, how can I take you to our house?' asked Kannabiran.

'Can't you come to the point without beating around the bush?' countered Sivakami.

'I can't, thangachi! There's a reason for that. When I was a young boy . . .'

'Please stop! The kumara chakravarthy left the monastery in a hurry. Is there any news?'

'Emissaries have arrived from Madurai.'

When Sivakami heard this, she was reminded of emissaries being sent to arrange a suitable wedding alliance for Mamallar. So, she asked anxiously, 'What news did the emissaries bring?'

'I don't pay attention to matters of the state, thangachi!' remarked Kannabiran.

Hearing this, Aayanar observed, 'That's a good practice, thambi! You must be extremely cautious when you are engaged in royal service. We should not heed matters that do not concern us.'

At that moment, the chariot was traversing the South Main Road, just in front of the palace entrance.

The palace occupied one entire side of the road. Sivakami observed the outer walls of the palace, the tower at the front entrance, the warriors who guarded the palace, the high walls that were visible inside the palace and its multiple storeys. She sighed deeply for a moment, thinking of the high walls that separated her and the prince who had captivated her.

38

Kamali

Behind the chakravarthy's palace at Kanchi was a large garden.

Adjacent to the garden's rear wall were a few small buildings. These were horse stables, chariot sheds and houses where the charioteers and gardeners lived.

The chariot which Kannabiran rode came to a halt in front of one of those houses. Hearing the sound of the chariot, a woman enthusiastically rushed out of the house.

As Kannabiran jumped out of the chariot, he announced, 'Kamali, see whom I have brought along!'

Kamali, who saw Sivakami alighting from the chariot, leapt forward and hugged her warmly.

At that point of time, an elderly man came from inside the house.

'Appa! Look who has come!' observed Kannabiran. That elderly man looked intently for a moment. He walked towards Aayanar saying, 'Please come, aiyya!'

The elderly man and Aayanar sat on the patio and continued talking. Sivakami and Kamali went inside the house.

Sivakami and Kamali were childhood friends. When Aayanar used to live in Kanchi, he and Kamali's parents were neighbours. Kamali was a year-and-a-half older than Sivakami. When Sivakami was a child, Kamali used to seat Sivakami on her lap, call her 'thangachi' and pamper her. Sivakami reciprocated, calling her 'Akka, akka!'

What started as a friendship between children deepened over time. When Aayanar shifted to his forest residence, Kamali used to visit them and stay there for months at a time.

Whenever Sivakami practised dancing, Kamali used to watch intently without batting an eyelid. She used to praise Sivakami's proficiency. Kamali used to pronounce, 'My sister has no peers in this universe!' Kamali was second only to Aayanar in encouraging Sivakami to pursue dance.

Kamali's father was a reputed horse trader in Kanchi. He used to import horses from several foreign countries, including Arabia. When ships carrying these imported horses arrived at the Mamallapuram harbour, he brought the horses to Kanchi. The head of the palace stables, Ashwabalar, and the chief of the Pallava army cavalry would be the first to inspect and buy the horses. Kamali's father would then sell the remaining horses to civilians.

Hence Ashwabalar used to often visit Kamali's father. Sometimes his son accompanied him. His son was Kannabiran.

When the two fathers discussed horse-trading, the son and daughter bartered their hearts. When the two families came to know of this, they solemnized Kannabiran's marriage with Kamali.

Their wedding had taken place a year and a half ago. Though Sivakami and Kamali had not met after the latter's marriage, not a day had passed without the two women thinking of each other.

After dinner, Aayanar and Ashwabalar lay down on the airy patio and discussed the impending war.

Inside the house, Sivakami and Kamali were lying down in the room adjacent to the palace garden and conversing. But they did not discuss the war. Kamali's married life was the primary topic of their conversation. The sound of their laughter was heard intermittently.

When it was about one-and-a-half jaamam since night set in, Aayanar called out from the patio, 'Sivakami! We need to leave before dawn. Enough of talking. Go to sleep!'

Kamali and Sivakami immediately closed their eyes and tried to sleep.

After some time, thinking that Sivakami was asleep, Kamali noiselessly woke up, opened the door and went to the next room.

* * *

Though Sivakami's eyes were closed, she was not asleep. Several thoughts rose within her like waves.

Kamali used to share with Sivakami her most intimate thoughts from the day she fell in love with Kannabiran. From the beginning, Kamali's love had been joyous. She had felt no sorrow or heartburn. Those days, Kamali's speech was filled with happiness and enthusiasm.

Sivakami realized that, even after marriage, the couple was extremely happy.

But why should her love be so different? She experienced so much sorrow, anger and distress.

Comparing Kamali's blissful love and her agonizing love, she concluded that the reason for her sorrow was falling in love with someone far above her social stature.

He is someone who one day will ascend the throne of the large empire. I am the daughter of a sculptor, who works on stones with a chisel. Falling in love with him was a big blunder. But who was the cause of this blunder?

He was the one who had pursued this humble sculptor's daughter. He was the one who had ignited the flame of love in an innocent girl, who used to wander about the forest happily, like a deer. Ah! That love had transformed into a major fire and scorched her body and soul.

Though Sivakami tossed and turned in the bed for some time, she was unable to sleep. She sat on the rear window seat of that room. As expected, the cool Pankuni breeze caressed her. The breeze did not blow in isolation. It brought along the fragrance of frangipani and jasmine from the palace garden.

The combined fragrance of frangipani and jasmine aroused old memories in Sivakami. She had dim memories of inhaling a fragrance like this and experiencing such agonizing ecstasy long ago. She fantasized that, though her lover who had captivated her heart was nearby, indescribable difficulties cast their dark shadow and prevented the two of them from coming together.

39

Kamali's Wish

Unable to bear the memories that gave her indescribable happiness and sorrow, Sivakami got up from her window seat. She opened the rear door of the room noiselessly and entered the garden. It was the third jaamam of the night then. Drenched in the half-moon light, the garden appeared to be a scene from a dream world.

Sivakami, who had stepped out with the intention of strolling around the garden, walked along the wall for some distance. She was surprised when she heard voices and stopped. Kamali and Kannabiran were conversing. Their voices could be clearly heard through the rear window of their room.

Unwilling to proceed in that direction, Sivakami wanted to turn around. It was then she heard the names 'Mamallar' and 'kumara chakravarthy' being uttered. Her legs refused to move. She stood in a corner by the wall and listened to their conversation.

'Is it surprising that the Pandya king has offered his daughter's hand in marriage to Mamallar? Wouldn't all kings on earth compete with each other to get their daughter married to Mamallar?' said Kamali.

'The maharani is desirous of getting Mamallar married early. She had arranged to send emissaries to the kings of three states. This did not materialize due to the impending war. Now that the Pandya king himself has sent an emissary offering his daughter in marriage, the maharani is extremely happy,' said Kannabiran.

'What happened after that?' asked Kamali.

'I took Mamallar to the palace. Immediately, an argument broke out between mother and son . . .'

'Argument! Why?'

'If someone even utters the word "marriage" to the kumara chakravarthy, he gets furious. "Is this why you sent for me so urgently? I rushed here thinking there may be some news from the battlefield," he told the maharani angrily! Kamali, shall I tell you a secret? It is a very important one. You will be stunned when you hear it!' said Kannan.

'Don't you know that you ought not to divulge secrets to women, Kanna?' asked Kamali teasingly.

'Oh! Are you a woman? I forgot!' said Kannan in jest.

'True! Even I forgot that you are a man, now that war is approaching.'

'Let the war begin. Then you will know the difference between male and female! You will prostrate before me sobbing and say, "Kanna! Don't go to the battlefield." I will ignore you and proceed . . .'

'Do you harbour such thoughts in your mind? If you do not go to the battlefield when the war begins, I myself will catch you by your neck and push you there. It seems that the kumara chakravarthy is refusing to get married after seeing you turn into a coward after marriage!'

'Do you think so, Kamali? Everyone thinks that the kumara chakravarthy is refusing to get married because of the imminent war. It's not so, Kamali!'

'Why not, Kanna?'

'There's another covert reason for Mamallar refusing to get married, Kamali. That involves your sister Sivakami!'

'What is that? How can there be a secret about my sister Sivakami that is not known to me? Beware if you say something slanderous.'

'There is nothing slanderous; it is something to be proud of! What will you give me if I tell you?'

'You first tell me the secret and then ask! One can determine the price only after examining the wares,' said Kamali.

'You must not cheat me afterwards! Kamali, the kumara chakravarthy of the Pallava empire, who is comparable to Arjuna for his valour, Manmadan for his good looks and Lord Krishna for his expertise in riding a chariot, has fallen in love with your sister, Sivakami!'

Only the syllable 'Ah!' escaped Kamali's mouth. She stood frozen with shock.

The syllable 'Ah!' pierced the heart of Sivakami, who stood outside listening. She was ashamed of concealing her love for so long from her dear friend Kamali, who trusted and loved her so much. The conversation inside the room continued.

'Kamali! Aren't you surprised by this news?' asked Kannabiran.

'What is so surprising? Haven't I told you that our kumara chakravarthy is intelligent? That's why he fell in love with my sister,' responded Kamali cleverly.

'Oh! Is that so? It seems as though you and your sister conferred before this act was committed. You ensnared me. You sister ensnared Mamallar himself!'

'What did you say?' asked Kamali angrily and started arguing with him. 'Did I come after you and ensnare you? Did I chase you at every nook and corner in the house, hold your hand firmly and plead, "My dear! If you don't have mercy on me, I will die!"? Was I the one who beseeched, "Please marry me"?'

'No, Kamali, you spread the net using your eyes! I myself came running and got caught in it!'

'Forget our story. Tell me how you came to know of Mamallar and my sister being in love?' asked Kamali.

'Ah! Only a snake can anticipate the movements of another snake! Only a thief can recognize another thief. Remember how I used to gaze at you while visiting your father's house those days. Mamallar is gazing at your sister in a similar fashion these days!'

'Is that all?'

'What other proof do you need? Didn't I mention that your sister fainted after dancing at Navukkarasar's monastery? Immediately, Mamallar came running and placed Sivakami's head on Aayanar's lap. Do you know how his hands and body were shivering then? I was suspicious till today. Now, I'm certain.'

Hearing this, Sivakami trembled. She felt that she would break down crying. Suppressing her emotions, she continued to listen to the conversation.

'You observed all this keenly; you are very clever! Mamallar is fortunate!' said Kamali.

'Did you say that Mamallar is fortunate? Do you know how many complications will arise because of this?'

'What complications will arise?'

'Do you think that the kumara chakravarthy's wedding is as straightforward as ours? There will be several considerations.'

'Kanna! My sister is no ordinary woman! Wouldn't people flock to marry Sivakami, just like the devas came to marry Damayanti? Damayanti condescended to marry a mortal like King Nala!'

'But Damayanti was a princess from a royal clan, Kamali!'

'My sister is equal to a thousand princesses, Kanna! Why don't you wait and watch! My wish will come true one day.'

'What is your wish, Kamali?'

'After this war is over, Mamallar's coronation will be held. Narasimha Chakravarthy will be taken in procession through the royal streets on a golden chariot and seated on a throne embellished with navaratnas. My sister Sivakami will be seated next to him akin to Indrani and Devendran. You will be riding the chariot majestically. I will watch this sight from the upper storey of the palace as your chariot reaches the main entrance of the palace. When the chariot comes to a halt before the palace, baskets of jasmine and frangipani will be showered on them. In the midst of all this, I will shower a basket of flowers on you. My desire is that all this should happen, Kanna!'

'Kamali, if your wish comes true, I will be extremely happy too,' said Kannan.

Sivakami returned to her room and lay on the bed. She was unable to control the tears that surged from the bottom of her heart.

In the fourth jaamam of the night, she tossed and turned, half asleep. The shadow-like figures she had previously seen in her mind's eye assumed form.

There were two branches to a shenbaga tree. Doves perched on the branches were frolicking. Suddenly, all the surrounding trees caught fire. The male dove flew away after telling the female dove, 'You stay here! I will return and rescue you!'

The female dove kept looking in the direction in which the male dove flew away. Will the male dove return? Will he rescue the female dove? The smoke which enveloped all four sides made it impossible to ascertain the fate of the female dove. Sivakami fantasized that the female dove in distress was her incarnation.

There was a change of scene in her dream. In a jasmine garden, a deer and a doe were playing. While playing, the doe hid behind a jasmine bush. Unable to find the doe, which was covered with jasmine buds, the deer continued to run, passing by the doe. Seeing this, the doe burst out laughing. When they were playing thus, the doe was amazed to see two stars glowing lustrously in a jasmine bush. Then she saw that they were not stars but firestones. The doe realized that the firestones were the eyes of a big tiger, and she was immobilized. The doe tried to call out to the deer. But no voice emanated from her throat.

What happened after this? Did the doe escape? Was she united with the deer? That was not known. Sivakami realized that it was she and not the doe that was trapped in such a dangerous situation.

40

Journey under Duress

Paranjyothi, who had departed from the Mahendra rest house at dawn, travelled all day and reached the viharam located at the confluence of the north Pennai and Papagni rivers at sunset.

A bikshu was standing at the entrance of the viharam. In the yellow evening sun, the bikshu's ochre robes shone like gold. Paranjyothi dismounted from the horse and approached the bikshu, who posed a question to him. Paranjyothi did not understand the language the bikshu spoke in, but he surmised that the bikshu was enquiring about him. Paranjyothi told him in Tamil that he was heading to Nagarajuna mountain and that Naganandi adigal had instructed him to stop here and ask for directions.

A change in the bikshu's face was perceptible when he heard the name Naganandi. He gestured to Paranjyothi to remain at the entrance and went inside. He returned after some time and escorted Paranjyothi into the viharam.

Paranjyothi observed that, unlike the royal viharam at Kanchi that was built of stone, wood and cement, this viharam was sculpted out of a hill. This viharam was not as large as the one in Kanchi, nor were the prayer articles found here as expensive. But the layouts of both viharams were similar. At the centre of the viharam was a hall in which the bikshus could conduct group prayers and meditate. On the wall made of rock at the back of the room was sculpted a large statue of Lord Buddha. The statue, the Bodhi tree and Gandharvas showering flowers on Lord Buddha were all sculpted out of rocks. Rows of decorative lamps were illuminated. Heaps of flowers of different colours arranged before Lord Buddha's statue were a feast to the eyes. The fragrance from the flowers and incense helped to calm one's thoughts.

On both sides of the hall, rooms carved out of rock served as accommodation for the bikshus and classrooms for the students. At one corner was a flight of stairs. The bikshu lead Paranjyothi up the staircase. Like the lower floor, the rooms on the upper floor were also carved out of rock. Paranjyothi was taken to a large room, where the senior-most bikshu was seated in padmasana.

Paranjyothi, guessing that this bikshu was the head of the monastery, performed a namaskaram and bowed before him. The bikshu chanted, 'Buddham saranam gacchami, Dharmam saranam gacchami, Sangam saranam gacchami' thrice while bowing to Lord Buddha. He then asked Paranjyothi in Tamil, 'My child, who are you? What is the purpose of your visit? Who sent you here?'

Paranjyothi explained in detail that Naganandi had sent him with an epistle.

'Where is the missive Naganandi sent? May I see it?' asked the bikshu.

'Please forgive me. Naganandi has commanded me to hand over the epistle to no one but Satyasraya,' said Paranjyothi.

A mysterious smile appeared on the bikshu's face when he heard the name Satyasraya. Though Paranjyothi observed this, he was unable to comprehend the import of that smile.

'Do act in accordance with Naganandi adigal's command. You stay here tonight. These days, dangers abound on the route to Sri Parvatham. Tonight, some warriors who are headed there may arrive. I will send you with them. Not only will they guide you, but they will also safely escort you there,' said the senior bikshu. He then gestured to another bikshu.

That bikshu escorted Paranjyothi away, served him food and showed him a room where he could lie down. As he had slept fitfully the previous night and had travelled a long distance that day, sound sleep overcame Paranjyothi as soon as he lay down.

* * *

Paranjyothi woke up with a start when he felt someone holding him by his shoulders and shaking him. The bikshu who had taken him into the viharam the previous day was trying to wake him up. The senior bikshu was standing next to him.

'Thambi, those going to the Nagarjuna mountain are departing now. You too must leave,' said the senior bikshu.

Paranjyothi stood up in a rush. He picked up the tube that contained the manuscript, which he'd kept beneath his headrest, fastened it around his waist and followed the bikshus to the entrance of the monastery.

In the dim light emitted by the rising sun, he observed that there were six horses beside his horse, and well-built warriors standing next to each one of them.

'These warriors are going to Sri Parvatham on an urgent task. If you go with them, you will reach there quickly through a shortcut,' remarked the senior bikshu.

Paranjyothi mounted the horse hesitantly, for he was troubled by some unknown factor. The horses rode swiftly westwards by the banks of the North Pennai River.

41

Army Camp

Once they had left the viharam, three of the warriors rode ahead of Paranjyothi and three followed him, thereby ensuring that he was always in their midst.

When it was morning, Paranjyothi carefully observed their appearance. They were strong, well-built men. These warriors must have been attached to some army, he thought. Their mission was an important war-related task. Why did that bikshu send him along with these warriors?

As time passed by, Paranjyothi became more and more confused. When he tried to race ahead of those warriors or follow them, they would not allow him to do so. They always ensured that he was in the middle. As he observed this, he was not sure if they were trying to guide him or had imprisoned him.

Paranjyothi knew that Sri Parvatham was located in the north, on the banks of the Krishna River. But these warriors were travelling westwards. He initially thought that they would travel for some time in that direction and then turn to the north. But that did not happen.

After travelling in this manner till noon, Paranjyothi wanted to ascertain if he was truly imprisoned. He turned his horse towards a north-bound road. The six warriors immediately surrounded him with lightning speed. Their spears were pointing towards his horse.

Just like a wick dipped in oil is illuminated as soon as it comes into contact with fire, the fury that was suppressed within Paranyothi was set ablaze. His blood boiled in anger.

He took out his spear and flung it at the man next to him.

Ah! How disappointing! The spear fell elsewhere, and the owner of the spear fell to the ground. Paranjyothi could not fathom how he was made to stand up. He saw there was a rope around him. One of the horsemen had made a loop out of a rope, hurled it at Paranjyothi and pulled him down.

When Paranjyothi was reminded that he had been defeated for the second time treacherously, shame and anger overcame him. His horse trotted away, retracing its steps, as though it had realized that its master had no more use for a horse.

Realizing that there was no way to escape, Paranjyothi resigned himself to his fate and did not do anything.

Three of the warriors dismounted from their horses and fastened Paranjyothi's hands to his back and bound him with a rope. They mounted him on the strongest and sturdiest of the six horses. One of the warriors sat behind him. The horses started riding westwards again.

One jaamam before sunset, Paranjyothi saw an awe inspiring sight ahead of him.

At that time, the path on which they were travelling was becoming steep as it led to the top of the plateau. A vast tract of flat landscape met the eye. An army camp that stretched up to the horizon was stationed there.

Thousands of elephants trained for war stood in rows like black hills. The white tents pitched amongst the elephants resembled white hills. Countless horses, camels, rams, chariots and carts dotted the landscape. Like ants that swarm a place strewn with sugar, lakhs of warriors were in the army camp. At certain places, they were in groups and at other places they were dispersed.

Several indecipherable sounds, like the roar of a tempestuous sea, could be heard at the army camp.

Seeing this, Paranjyothi appreciatively exclaimed, 'Ah!'

Paranjyothi thought that it was the Pallava army camp that lay ahead of him. He then felt an ardour that made him forget his confined state.

The ardour was fuelled by his desire to join the army that was preparing to fight a valorous battle. Paranjyothi unambiguously realized at that instant his life's mission, just like lightning illuminating the path for a traveller who had lost his way at night. He was not born to write with a stylus on a palm leaf, to sing devotional songs, to sculpt boulders with a chisel or to paint pictures on a wall! He realized that he was born to wield swords and spears in the battlefield, decapitate the heads of foes, fling spears at their chests, swim in rivers of blood, overcome foes with the background sound of conches being blown to signify victory and to be lauded as 'the bravest of the brave'.

This thought gave Paranjyothi tremendous joy. The imposing image of Mahendra chakravarthy, whom he had seen at Aayanar's house while hiding behind the Buddha statue, appeared before his eyes.

The stately Mahendra chakravarthy would be the commander-in-chief of this army whose flags were fluttering in the sky. These people would take him to Mahendra chakravarthy.

Paranjyothi decided that as soon as he was in the chakravarthy's presence, he would prostrate before him and plead, 'Prabhu! Pallavendra! Please permit this ignorant rustic youth to join your formidable army!' He had ceased to care about paintings, additives, Aayanar and Naganandi.

As Paranjyothi neared the army camp harbouring such thoughts, doubts clouded his enthusiasm. He began to wonder if it was the Pallava army camp that was stationed here.

The flag of the Pallava empire bore the rishabha insignia. But the flags here, bearing the symbol of a varaha, a boar, presented a harsh sight!

Probably, this is the Vatapi army, he thought. *Is this the army that is about to invade the Pallava empire? Is the army that is about to attack the Pallava kingdom so enormous and strong?*

As soon as they reached the entrance of the army camp, the warriors alighted from their horses, brought Paranjyothi down and escorted him inside.

As Paranjyothi walked through the army camp, his earlier doubts were confirmed. The appearance of the soldiers at the army camp and the language they spoke confirmed without doubt that this army could not be the Pallava army.

'Ah! This is the enemy's army camp! It's unfortunate I am caught here. It seems that there is no way to escape.' As Paranjyothi was thinking thus, he froze in shock and the ropes that bound his body hurt him much more than before. He faltered because he was disheartened and was in pain. So, the warriors accompanying him dragged him along.

At that point of time, Paranjyothi saw a familiar figure walking towards him. Paranjyothi realized that it was Vajrabahu, his travel companion of two days before.

At first, Paranjyothi felt a little happy. Then he thought, 'This man is the sole reason for my current condition!'

Vajrabahu seemed to be surprised at Paranjyothi's presence there. He asked, 'Thambi, why are you in this state?' He had a word with the warriors escorting Paranjyothi and then said, 'Thambi, don't be scared! Tell King Satyasraya Pulikesi what actually transpired. No harm will befall you.'

It was the glint in Vajrabahu's eyes rather than his words that gave Paranjyothi courage.

42

Satyasrayan

King Pulikesi ruled the vast empire that stretched from the Narmada River in the north to the Tungabhadra River in the south, with Vatapi as its capital. He was regarded as a peerless warrior in Bharata Kandam those days. To understand him, it is necessary to know his antecedents.

When Pulikesi and his brother were children, they were subject to their uncle Mangalesan's cruelty. They escaped from Mangalesan's prison and lived in hiding for a long time in a dense forest. The untold hardships they suffered in the forest hardened their bodies and souls and transformed them into accomplished and ruthless warriors.

At the opportune time, Pulikesi came out of hiding, overthrew his uncle and ascended the Vatapi throne. Then he started expanding the borders of the Vatapi empire with the assistance of his brave brothers. He expanded his empire northwards till it reached the Narmada River. His army had to combat the forces of the till-then unchallenged emperor of Utthara Bharata, Harshavardhana.

A war was waged on both banks of the Narmada River for several years. Though the Vatapi troops fought bravely, as Harshavardhana's army was constantly replenished, they could not achieve a definitive victory. In this situation, Harshavardhana himself decided to come to the battlefield accompanied by a massive army. Pulikesi realized that fighting Harshavardhana was akin to banging himself against the Vindhya mountain. Pulikesi called for a truce. Harshavardhana, who was a great soul, immediately accepted the truce, lauded Pulikesi's gallant acts, and acknowledged Pulikesi as the emperor of the region to the south of the Narmada River.

Then, Pulikesi turned his attention southwards. The key people who diverted his attention to the south were the Jain monks.

As the Jains had assisted Pulikesi in ascending the Chalukya throne, their monks enjoyed an exalted status in Vatapi. The Jain monks mediated the marriage between the daughter of the king of Gangapadi, Durvineethan, and Pulikesi's brother, Vishnuvardhanan.

When the Kanchi emperor, Mahendra chakravarthy, renounced Jainism and embraced Saivism, Jains all over the country were enraged. This was because Kanchi, which was renowned for its education, had also served as the seat of Jain gurus for a long time. The area beyond the river Vehavathi at Kanchi was known as 'Jinakanchi', the Jain quarters. The Jain seminary at Patalipuram, a town located at the estuary of the South Pennai River, was the finest in Dakshina Bharata. The Jains could not tolerate the dominance of Saivism over Jainism in this region.

Their instigation, coupled with Pulikesi's desire to become the undisputed emperor, fuelled his decision to invade Dakshina Bharata, leading an army of unprecedented size.

When the army embarked on its invasion of the south, the Jain monks too accompanied the soldiers, thinking that they would enter Kanchi with trumpets proclaiming their victory, and would teach Mahendrar a lesson.

But they soon understood the difference between a capital city and an army camp, and between the emperor Pulikesi and the commander-in-chief Pulikesi. At Vatapi, Jain monks like Pujya Pathar and Ravikeerthi commanded more respect than Emperor Pulikesi himself. But on the battlefield, nobody gave them a second look. After Pulikesi overruled their advice to refrain from burning Vyjayanthi Pattinam, they were reluctant to remain on the battlefield. After arguing for a while with Pulikesi, they took leave of him and returned.

***

In a large tent pitched under a flag bearing the varaha insignia, King Pulikesi was majestically seated on an ivory throne, wearing his crown. Seven to eight people were sitting on an ornate carpet spread in front of the throne. It was evident from their appearance that they were army commanders and people holding senior positions. Their eyes displayed both fear and devotion as they looked at Pulikesi.

The language that Pulikesi and his commanders spoke was a combination of Prakrit and Tamil.

'What were the Digambar monks thinking when they accompanied us? How can we win if we conduct the war in accordance with their wishes?' said Pulikesi.

'It is good that they left. If they come with us, we cannot wage war. We would have to build temples, monasteries and stupas along the way!' said one commander.

Everyone burst out laughing.

When the laughter subsided, another commander said, 'We have sent the Jain monks away. But this war is being conducted in accordance with the bikshu's wishes.' He then looked at Pulikesi.

'Ah! That's another matter. We have not suffered any loss by heeding the bikshu's advice. Nothing has gone wrong,' said Pulikesi.

Then he pointedly looked at one person sitting in front of him and said, 'It seems that our spies are working extremely efficiently. Instead of our spies tracing the bikshu's messenger, the messenger himself is coming to meet us!' When he said this, his naturally harsh tone sounded even more abrasive.

The head of the spies lowered his eyes for a moment. Then he looked up at Pulikesi and said, 'A mistake has been committed. The men I had sent have not returned . . . ' As he was talking, people entered the tent. He turned around, looked at them, and exclaimed, 'Ah! They have come!'

The warriors, having immobilized Paranjyothi by binding ropes around his body, dragged him along as they entered the tent.

Seeing this sight, Pulikesi asked, 'What is this? Who is this boy?' His words boomed like thunder in Paranjyothi's ears.

43

Mysterious Message

The king of kings, Pulikesi, was a man with a gaunt physique. His face reflected his steely determination and cruel, ruthless character. His reddened hawk-like eyes appeared to look into the future.

Shock and déjà vu gripped those who saw Pulikesi for the first time. Such a face, with its combination of dignity and cruelty, and eyes displaying both wisdom and anger, could only be that of Yama Dharma Raja.

Paranjyothi reached the same conclusion.

The leader of the warriors who had imprisoned Paranjyothi bowed to Satyasraya Pulikesi. He then detailed what had transpired from the time the head of the viharam at the banks of the North Pennai River had asked them to take the youth to the emperor.

Pulikesi lost his patience before he could finish and thundered angrily, 'That's all right! Who is he? Why have you brought him here?'

The leader of the warriors responded in a quivering voice, 'This boy says that he has a message from Naganandi adigal for Satyasrayar. Here is the epistle.' He then took the missive from Paranjyothi and offered it to Pulikesi.

Pulikesi opened the communiqué and read it attentively. Signs of surprise and confusion appeared on his face. Even after reading the missive twice, there were no signs of clarity.

As Pulikesi was reading the message, the commanders seated in front of him continued looking at him.

Paranjyothi was exceedingly confused. When he had embarked on this journey with Naganandi's missive, he had not even imagined that he would be captured by enemies and presented before the adversary king. His meeting Vajrabahu at the enemy camp, who had mentioned in passing, 'Tell Satyasraya Pulikesi what actually transpired!' further heightened his confusion.

Paranjyothi felt dizzy when he remembered Naganandi's words. 'You have to give this communiqué to Satyasrayar. Do not hand it over to anyone else. You may meet Satyasrayar on the way itself. You cannot predict the disguise he may assume. Don't be surprised with his masquerade when you meet him!' As Paranjyothi thought, 'Is the Satyasrayar Naganandi referred to the king of Vatapi, Pulikesi? Didn't the epistle pertain to the Ajantha paint additive? Or am I trapped in a major and mysterious treachery?' He was thoroughly baffled.

Pulikesi raised his head, astonished, and asked his commanders, 'Do you know what is written in this missive?' Immediately, he himself responded, stating, 'You will never be able to guess,' and laughed aloud.

His laughter came to an abrupt halt just like thunder ceasing. He then looked at Paranjyothi, who stood bound amidst the guards. Pulikesi's hawk-like eyes seemed to pierce through Paranjyothi's heart.

Pulikesi posed a volley of questions to him in a harsh tone. 'Boy! Tell me the truth! Who are you? Where have you come from? Who gave you this message? Are you aware of its contents?' As Paranjyothi was unable to understand even one of those questions, he stood silently.

But Pulikesi's anger intensified. Seeing this, one of the commanders said, 'Probably this boy is deaf!'

Another one said, 'He is dumb!'

Yet another one said, 'That's not the case. He probably does not understand our language. That's why he is staring!'

Then Pulikesi said, 'Yes, that must be the case. That's a difficulty after the Jain monks left. Had they been present, they would have translated any language. That's all right. Imprison him. We will attend to him later!' Suddenly, he said, 'No, let him be here. Go and fetch the warrior Vajrabahu who was here some time ago!'

After a man was sent to fetch Vajrabahu, Pulikesi told the commanders, 'Do you know what is written in this message? Listen to this wonder! We should share the secret of the Ajantha paintings with the bearer of this missive. I was unable to extract the secret of the paints from the bikshus when I had lived in the Ajantha caves for two years. The bikshus safeguard the secret of the paintings so carefully. But this epistle instructs us to share the secret with this boy. The handwriting resembles our bikshu's handwriting. What do you think of this, Maitreyar?' Pulikesi handed over the communiqué to the leader of the spies as he was talking.

Maitreyar took the missive and read it carefully. Then he told the emperor, 'Satyasraya, there seems to be a hidden message in this epistle. If we interrogate this boy in the appropriate manner, the truth will be known!'

'How smart, Maitreyar! Even if we interrogate this boy, what he says is of use to us only if we understand him! That's why I called for Vajrabahu,' said Pulikesi.

Vajrabahu entered the tent even as Pulikesi spoke. He bowed before Pulikesi and asked, 'Rajathi raja, do you have any other command?'

Vajrabahu turned around, looked at Paranjyothi intently, and said, 'Ah! This boy! I saw him the day before yesterday at the Mahendra rest house! I was doubtful as soon as I saw him. I questioned him. But the boy was tight-lipped, he did not respond!'

'You question him now. If he does not respond, we will make him do so,' said the king of Vatapi.

'King of kings, he seems to be a true-blue warrior. We cannot extract any information by threatening him. I myself will question him.' Saying this, Vajrabahu looked at Paranjyothi and asked, 'Thambi! Didn't I tell you earlier? Tell Satyasrayar what actually happened! Don't be scared. I will ensure you escape.'

Paranjyothi replied, 'Aiyya, I am not afraid. Why should I be scared? There can be no greater loss than one's life, can there? Naganandi bikshu asked me to hand over this epistle to Satyasrayar at Nagarjuna mountain. If, as you say, this message is meant for him, let him retain it and give me a written response. I will receive the response and return. If the missive is not meant for him, he should return it to me. I have nothing more to say.'

Vajrabahu told Pulikesi, 'King of kings, this boy claims that it was Naganandi bikshu who gave him the communiqué and that it has a message relating to the Ajantha paint additive. May I see that epistle?'

Pulikesi handed it over to Vajrabahu and said, 'Nothing is evident from this missive. You read it yourself.'

Vajrabahu attentively read the message for some time and then asked, 'Prabhu! Isn't the head of the Buddha sangramam at Nagarjuna mountain Satyasraya Bikshu?'

'Yes. So what?'

'Probably this missive is meant for him.'

'Maybe, but what is the necessity for Naganandi to send him such a message?'

'Prabhu, after reading this message I recollect something Naganandi bikshu had said. He had mentioned that he also needs to send a message to your brother who is now invading the kingdom of Vengi located on the banks of River Krishna. Probably this communiqué has a message for your brother, King Vishnuvardhanan.'

Hearing this, Pulikesi's face glowed. He said, 'Vajrabahu, you are very astute. You should stay with me. You can assist me in several tasks.'

He held discussions with his commanders for some time. He then commanded, 'I would anyway have to send a message to Vishnuvardhanan. Let nine warriors depart with the missive. Send this boy along with them. If my brother too is unable to comprehend the message, instruct them to behead the boy immediately!' He then looked at Vajrabahu and ordered, 'Communicate this to the boy.'

Vajrabahu told Paranjyothi, 'Thambi, nine warriors are heading to Nagarjuna mountain tomorrow morning. They will take you along. You don't have to worry at all. I will meet you on the way tomorrow night.'

Paranjyothi, whose heart and face lit up, said, 'If I have to travel with you, I am willing to come to hell. I am so eager to listen to your stories!'

Pulikesi asked, 'What does the boy say?'

Vajrabahu responded, 'The boy is extremely sharp. He is asking for the missive to be returned, if it is not meant for you. There is a proverb in Tamil which states that a fledgling knows no fear!'

Pulikesi laughed and said, 'Is that so? Good! Let's return the epistle to the boy. For now, undo the ropes that bind him!'

The missive was returned to Paranjyothi and the ropes that restrained him were also untied. Then they took him away from the emperor's assembly.

The following day, Paranjyothi, surrounded by nine horsemen, crossed a narrow mountain pass and, at dusk, reached a dilapidated old house. An old man was sitting at the entrance of that house. That old man, whose hair and beard had greyed, appeared to have no concerns regarding worldly matters. He was fingering the rosary he held. He did not even pay attention to the ten horses coming to a halt in front of his house.

The leader of the soldiers asked the old man something, to which he responded in one or two words, and continued rolling his rosary beads.

The soldiers decided to spend the night in that dilapidated house. They arranged for four people amongst them to stand guard for four jaamams.

Paranjyothi, who was the most fatigued of them all, went to sleep as soon as he lay down. Just before falling asleep, he thought, 'Vajrabahu had mentioned that he would meet me tonight. How can we meet now?'

Paranjyothi had a dream that night too. Pulikesi's harsh hawk-like eyes pierced his heart for a moment and then he commanded, 'Fetch an elephant to trample him!' Paranjyothi flung his spear at the approaching elephant and fled. The elephant chased him. It finally neared him, and as soon as the elephant's trunk touched him, Paranjyothi looked around, startled. The elephant's face transformed to that of the old man who was seated at the entrance of the house and the trunk became the old man's hand.

When Paranjyothi realized that he was not dreaming and that the old man was waking him up, he immediately got up.

44

Enigmatic Old Man

Paranjyothi, aided by the dim moonlight streaming in through the window, observed that the old man was holding a spear and gesturing to Paranjyothi to accompany him. When Paranjyothi delayed slightly, the old man tightened his grip on Paranjyothi's right hand. As Paranjyothi recollected an old incident, he took the spear that enigmatic old man was holding and leapt up.

Both of them exited the house through the backyard. Paranjyothi noticed that his horse and another horse were ready with their saddles fastened. Both of them mounted the horses.

The old man's horse leapt forward, as Paranjyothi had expected. The old man was doing something, with his back towards Paranjyothi. So, Paranjyothi held back the reins of his horse.

The old man, who was delaying, asked Paranjyothi, 'Thambi! Do you recognize me?'

'I was initially deceived by your beard. When you held my hand, I recognized that you are the gallant Vajrabahu, who is not scared of ghosts,' said Paranjyothi. When the old man looked around, laughing aloud, the grey beard had disappeared from his face. The clean-shaven face was that of the brave Vajrabahu.

When Vajrabahu asked, 'Think and tell me. Are you willing to come with me?' Paranjyothi responded, 'I am willing to come. But you don't seem to have any intention of leaving this place.'

'Why do you say that?'

'If you speak so loudly, won't they wake up?'

'I am speaking loudly with the express intention of waking them up. Should Vajrabahu, who is a descendant of Vikranthan, bear the ignominy of fleeing away from sleeping men?' Saying this, Vajrabahu thought of something and laughed aloud.

On hearing the sounds of horse hooves and conversation, the man guarding the house in the front came running to the backyard. Seeing two men mounted on horses riding away, he exclaimed, 'Oh!' and ran into the house. The soldiers inside the house woke up immediately. There was a commotion when he told them about the escape.

Vajrabahu and Paranjyothi retraced the path that led to the dilapidated house. But Vajrabahu intentionally tightened the reins of his horse and slowed it down. He also stopped from time to time. When Paranjyothi enquired about the delay, he asked, 'Shouldn't we give time for the Chalukyas to catch up with us? What if they lose their way . . . ?'

'So what if they lose their way?' asked Paranjyothi.

'There is a mountain pass at a short distance from here. Did you notice that there was a temple dedicated to Durga Devi there?'

'No.'

'How could you have observed it? All your attention must have been at Thiruvengadu . . .'

'What did you say?'

'When I crossed the Durga Devi temple yesterday, I had vowed to sacrifice the lives of nine humans at dawn. If they lose their way, how can I fulfil my vow?'

Though Paranjyothi heard the old man's words, they did not register in his mind.

He was in a state of shock. Ever since he had left Thirusengattankudi, he had travelled a long distance and witnessed amazing incidents. Amidst all this action, his heart was regularly visiting Thiruvengadu. He could not understand how the deceptive Vajrabahu had come to know this.

Vajrabahu and Paranjyothi reached the mountain pass when dawn was breaking brightly. The path down which they travelled narrowed down at this point and was flanked by perpendicular walls of rock on both sides. As soon as they crossed the mountain pass, the wall of rock continued on one side and there was a deep ravine on the other.

When they reached this spot, Vajrabahu stopped his horse and made Paranjyothi follow suit.

A cool morning breeze was gently blowing through the mountain pass. Along with the sonorous chirping of birds, the distant sound of horses approaching was heard.

'Thambi, I am asking you again. Please let me know before the Chalukya soldiers arrive. Are you willing to accompany me?' Vajrabahu asked.

'Now that I have come with you, how can I return?'

'If you are unwilling to come with me, you may return and join them even now.'

'After joining them . . .'

'You can follow them to their destination.'

'Where are they going?'

'They think that they are going to Nagarjuna mountain. In truth, they are going to Yama Loka!'

'Who is going to send them there?'

'If you so desire, both of us can. If not, I will send them there.'

Paranjyothi thought for a moment and then asked, 'Where are you going?'

'To the Pallava army camp.'

'Ah! Just as I thought!' exclaimed Paranjyothi.

'How did you know?'

'I was thinking the whole of yesterday and deduced it.'

'What else did you deduce?'

'I realized that you are a spy of the Kanchi chakravarthy.'

'Thambi! I took you lightly. You're extremely clever.'

'Aiyya! If I come with you, will I be enlisted in the Pallava army?'

'You will definitely be enlisted. Should one be compensated to eat sugarcane? The Pallava army is fortunate to enlist a warrior like you!' said Vajrabahu.

Paranjyothi did not respond to this and kept quiet for some time.

'Appane, what are you thinking about?' asked Vajrabahu.

'What am I supposed to do with this message?'

'Throw it down the ravine there into the river flowing below! There is no use for it anymore.'

'Won't Naganandi and Aayanar be disappointed?'

'Naganandi will be extremely disappointed!' Saying this, Vajrabahu laughed aloud.

'Why are you laughing?'

'Because the bikshu handed over the missive to a Kumbakarnan like you!'

'Aiyya! Please pardon me. I will go to Nagarjuna mountain, hand over Naganandi's epistle and come to the Pallava army camp.'

'Pointless chore, appane! The message Naganandi gave you was dedicated to Agni!'

'What are you saying!'

'I said that Naganandi's missive was burnt in fire.'

'No, I have it with me!'

'That's the communiqué I wrote, thambi!'

'I suspected this!' Saying this, Paranjyothi threw the epistle into the ravine. 'The other night, you had added an intoxicating substance to the lamp. After putting me to sleep, you appropriated the message. Is that correct?'

'Your mind is as sharp as the tip of your spear!' said Vajrabahu.

Paranjyothi looked up at Vajrabahu in an amazed and devoted manner and asked, 'Aiyya! What was written in the communiqué Naganandi gave me?'

'It had asked Pulikesi to immediately advance to Kanchi and crown himself as the emperor of Dakshina Bharata!'

'Oh! Did I carry a missive bearing such a treacherous message? How foolish of me!'

'Don't regret the past. The Chalukya soldiers are swiftly galloping towards Yama Loka. What are you going to do?' asked Vajrabahu.

'I will act according to your wishes!'

'Both of us will stand on either side of the mountain pass. Aim your spear at the chest of the soldier who comes first. Then use this sword to fight to the best of your abilities.' Saying this, Vajrabahu gave Paranjyothi one of the two swords he had.

Paranjyothi eagerly received the sword and stood prepared for his maiden combat.

45

Mountain Pass

Two nazhigai after sunrise, the mountain pass presented a gory sight. The red rays of the rising sun accentuated the carnage evident from the dark, blood-soaked rocks. The corpses of nine soldiers either with severed limbs, or with broken skulls, or with severe injuries on their bodies, lay in that mountain pass.

Vajrabahu was moving around these corpses. When he turned them over and examined them closely, it seemed as though he was frantically searching for something.

Paranjyothi was sitting on a rock some distance away. Extreme fatigue and disgust were apparent on his face. He was leaning against the rock, sword in hand. Beside him lay a blood-soaked spear.

The just concluded gruesome incident unfolded itself in his mind. Paranjyothi had sent three of the Chalukya soldiers, and Vajrabahu, five soldiers, to the abode of Yama. The ninth warrior, who had been farther away, had tried to ride away without fighting.

Then Vajrabahu had flung his sword, which found its mark on the fleeing soldier's back. He too had fallen dead. Paranjyothi, who had admired Vajrabahu's bravery till then, was repulsed by this incident. He was itching to ask Vajrabahu if it was valorous to kill a fleeing man from the rear.

Suddenly, he heard Vajrabahu exclaim, 'Ah!' and he turned around. Vajrabahu was reading a message.

Then Vajrabahu quickly came close to the rock on which Paranjyothi was sitting and mounted his horse. When he observed Paranjyothi still sitting, he asked, 'Thambi, aren't you coming?'

Paranjyothi shot a look at Vajrabahu that conveyed disappointment and disgust, and lowered his head again.

Vajrabahu rode up next to Paranjyothi and said, 'Appane, you fought like an expert warrior. You skilfully killed three Chalukya warriors who fought like demons. I am thinking of asking the Pallava army commander to appoint you as the head of the Pallava cavalry. What is the reason for your exhaustion and sorrow?'

Paranjyothi neither responded nor looked up. He turned away and looked eastwards towards the sun shining brightly on the mountain, as though he did not want to look at Vajrabahu.

Vajrabahu rode closer to Paranjyothi and said, 'Thambi, when I see you in this condition, do you know who I am reminded of? At the Kurukshetra war, both the armies stood on the battlefield, prepared to fight. When the war was about to begin, Arjuna threw away his bow saying, "I neither desire the war nor the kingdom. I cannot fight this war." He fell down in sorrow. You now resemble Arjuna.'

As soon as Paranjyothi heard the name Arjuna, he looked at Vajrabahu. The sorrow in his eyes was replaced by a glimmer. When Vajrabahu paused, he asked eagerly, 'What happened after that?'

'Fortunately for Arjuna, Lord Krishna was his charioteer. The Supreme Being said, "Arjuna! Get up! It is the dharma of a Kshatriya to engage in battle. Pick up your bow!" His advice to Arjuna is covered in eighteen chapters. On account of this, Arjuna overcame his weariness and was motivated again . . .' Saying this, Vajrabahu paused.

'Then?' asked Paranjyothi.

'Then what? Arjuna picked up the Gandivaand Krishna blew his conch, the Panchajanyam. The Mahabharata war began.'

'What happened in the war?' asked Paranjyothi.

'What happened? If I stand here relating the story of the Mahabharata war, what will happen to the war that is about to break out?' Saying this, Vajrabahu turned his horse around and started ascending the mountain path.

Paranjyothi leapt up holding the spear and sword and mounted his horse. Soon, he caught up with Vajrabahu.

Vajrabahu turned around and said, 'Thambi, have you reached? You look as though you intend to fight with me. Is that so?'

'Don't be scared. Even if I were to fight you, I will not stab you from behind! I will face you and fight! I am not courageous enough to kill a fleeing enemy from the rear!' said Paranjyothi in a bitter tone.

Vajrabahu kept quiet for some time and then said, 'Appane, do you know what would have happened had I not killed the fleeing soldier?'

'What would have happened?'

'The massive Vatapi army we saw will reach the gates of Kanchi within a month. Didn't I tell you about the fate of Vyjayanthi Pattinam?'

'Will Kanchi meet the same fate as Vyjayanthi? Where has the Pallava army gone? Where has Mahendra chakravarthy gone?'

'That's the mystery, thambi! No one knows where Mahendra chakravarthy went after leaving Kanchi! It seems that he has not reached the Pallava army camp yet,' said Vajrabahu.

Paranjyothi kept quiet for some time and then said, 'Aiyya, please tell me what Arjuna did next.'

46

Pulikesi's Love

Vajrabahu and Paranjyothi travelled non-stop through barren mountains, dry river beds filled with white sand and villages surrounded by mango groves where parrots abounded. Sometimes, Vajrabahu related heroic tales from the Mahabharata war to Paranjyothi.

Listening to Vajrabahu's description of Arjuna's skill with the bow, Abhimanyu's unparalleled heroism and the miracles Bheema performed with his mace, Paranjyothi got goosebumps. He fantasized that he had fought along with the Pandavas in the Kurukshetra war. Unconsciously, his hands strung a bow, flung spears at foes, and skilfully wielded a sword.

Sometimes, Vajrabahu would be immersed in deep thought. Then he would not respond to Paranjyothi's queries. He would ride at breakneck speed, irrespective of whether he was riding through steep paths, ditches, forests or water bodies. During such times, Paranjyothi found it difficult to keep pace with him.

Vajrabahu also used to speak of the Vatapi army's invasion and the danger facing the Pallava empire. Then, his tone gave away how worried he was. When they passed through peaceful, picturesque villages, he used to say, 'Ah! I shudder to think what will become of these villages shortly.'

Vajrabahu used to sigh whenever he saw large banyan trees with widespread branches that provided cool shade and verdant groves. 'When we travel through these parts again, I don't know if we will see this greenery!' he said.

When Paranjyothi insisted on knowing the reason for this surprising concern, Vajrabahu said, 'Appane, you have not seen the entire Vatapi army camp. I saw it! I feel like weeping when I think of the gigantic horde of elephants and these fertile groves!'

Paranjyothi said, 'I have seen people who care for fellow human beings and animals. I have never seen anyone shed tears for plants!'

'When I am concerned about flora, I also think of mankind. Thambi, a man's life is largely dependent on trees. In regions where there is lush growth of trees, rainfall is abundant. Rains fill the dams. Water levels rise in the rivers. People will be prosperous. If all the trees in a region are felled, rainfall will diminish. Famines are bound to break out. But how can you, a native of Chola Nadu through which the Kaveri River flows, realize all this?' said Vajrabahu.

'True, aiyya! I never realized the importance of lush green trees before. But what is the connection between what you just said and the Vatapi army?' asked Paranjyothi.

'Do you know how much food an elephant consumes in one day?'

'I don't know, aiyya.'

'Even if an elephant eats six measures of rice, nine bunches of bananas, twenty-five coconuts and half the leaves on a banyan tree, it will not be satiated!'

'Amma!' exclaimed Paranjyothi.

'After all this, the elephant has the capacity to consume its mahout too! But as elephants are herbivores, they do not eat their mahouts!'

Paranjyothi laughed and then asked, 'How many such elephants are there in the Vatapi army?'

'Fifteen thousand elephants, appane! If all these elephants came up to Kanchi and returned, all the fertile regions they pass through would turn barren.'

'Why do you keep saying that the Vatapi army will advance up to Kanchi?'

'Who can stop fifteen thousand elephants and a five-lakh-strong infantry from advancing, thambi? Only God can stop this army!'

When Paranjyothi remarked, 'I now realize why the Kanchi fort is secured thus,' Vajrabahu laughed sarcastically.

'Why are you laughing, aiyya?' asked Paranjyothi.

'Even I thought at one point of time that the Kanchi fort was extremely well protected. But now I know how wrong I was.'

'Why? Isn't the Kanchi fort adequately protected?' asked Paranjyothi. He remembered Naganandi taking him out of the fort through a secret tunnel.

'I am amused when I think of the Vatapi elephants banging against the fort gates after consuming liquor. The gates will be shattered to smithereens,' said Vajrabahu.

'How amazing! Do elephants consume liquor?'

'We could not convert elephants into carnivores. But we were able to train them to consume liquor. The

Vatapi army has brought large pots of liquor loaded on to thousands of carts. Apparently they are going to feed the elephants liquor and make them plow into the gates of the fort!'

'This is uncivilized warfare!' said Paranjyothi.

'War itself is uncivilized, thambi,' said Vajrabahu.

'You cannot categorize all warfare as uncivilized. Can the war which Mahendra chakravarthy is fighting to protect the country be called uncivilized?' said Paranjyothi.

'Don't mention Mahendra chakravarthy's name within my earshot! I'm infuriated that he ignored national security and spent his time in music and dance!'

Paranjyothi observed Vajrabahu's face intently and said, 'In that case, do you think it's impossible to safeguard the Kanchi fort?'

'If the Vatapi army were to march directly to the Kanchi fort, even God cannot protect it!'

'But it won't advance in that fashion, will it?'

'That's why I aimed the spear at the fleeing soldier and killed him. I gave a message to Pulikesi purportedly from Naganandi. If Pulikesi does not doubt its authenticity, Kanchi may be saved.'

'What was written in the communiqué you handed over, aiyya?'

'Thambi, I don't have to lie if you don't ask me about it!' Vajrabahu repeated the words that Paranjyothi had said to him once.

Paranjyothi remained silent for some time and then asked, 'As a result of your message, will the Chalukya army return to Vatapi without marching up to Kanchi?'

'Appane, had you seen the avarice in Pulikesi's eyes when the word Kanchi was uttered, you would not pose this question. Thinking that I am a descendant of Achutha Vikranthan, Pulikesi revealed his intentions to me . . .'

'Who is Achutha Vikranthan?' Paranjyothi interjected. He was extremely eager to know every subject in its entirety.

'Haven't you heard of Achutha Kallapal, who ruled an independent kingdom that was flanked by the Chola and Pandya empires two hundred years ago? Pulikesi believes that I am a descendant of Achutha Kallapal. He asked me, "Have you seen the city of Kanchi?" I replied in the affirmative. When I described Kanchi at Pulikesi's behest, the excitement that appeared on his face had to be seen to be believed. The lust that a cat feels on seeing a mouse was visible in Pulikesi's eyes. Do you know what Ravana said when he saw Sita, thambi? It seems he said, "If you don't love me, I will consume you for breakfast." Similarly, Pulikesi may be desirous of either ruling Kanchi or submitting it to Agni. Only God can rescue Kanchi from Pulikesi's destructive love.' Saying this, Vajrabahu lapsed into a long silence.

47

End of Journey

At sunset, they rode around the bend of a mountain path and the Pallava army camp came into sight. Only when Paranjyothi saw the Pallava army camp did he realize that Vajrabahu's concerns were not unfounded.

The difference between the Vatapi army camp and the Pallava army camp was stark.

'Thambi, do you see the army camp?' asked Vajrabahu.

'I do, aiyya!'

'Are you still confident that the Pallava army will win?'

'It will definitely win, aiyya! There is no doubt!' said Paranjyothi confidently.

'How are you so sure?'

'The Pallava army is backed by righteousness. Besides, Mahendra chakravarthy is with the army.'

'You seem to have tremendous confidence in Mahendra chakravarthy,' observed Vajrabahu.

'Yes, aiyya.'

'Have you seen the Pallava chakravarthy, thambi?'

'I have seen him twice. I saw him once when I was hiding behind the Buddha statue at the sculptor Aayanar's house. Another time, I saw him in the middle of the night in disguise. Then, the chakravarthy more or less resembled you. He also sported a big moustache like you.'

'True! I too have heard that Mahendra chakravarthy strolls around the city in disguise. People have mistaken me for the chakravarthy and vice versa.'

'I don't harbour such doubts, aiyya!'

'That's all right. You have seen both the Vatapi and Pallava armies; are you still desirous of enlisting with the Pallava army, thambi?'

'I am not just desirous but am zealous to join the Pallava army. It's a pity we're whiling away time by standing here and talking.'

'In that case, let me take leave of you!'

'What? Are you going away, leaving me here?'

'Yes, I will go in first and inform the Pallava chakravarthy about you. He may deign to send for you. Till then, you have to wait outside the army camp.'

'Is the chakravarthy at the army camp? You said that there was no news of the chakravarthy after he left Kanchi!'

'He may have reached by now.'

'Aiyya, I am desirous of seeing the chakravarthy face to face just once. You must help me!' said Paranjyothi eagerly.

'Why are you so keen to see the chakravarthy?' asked Vajrabahu.

'I will request him to hand over the task of safeguarding the Kanchi fort to me!'

'Oh! Aren't you the brave man who hurled the spear at the mad elephant? It seems that you wish to protect Kanchi in the same manner as you saved Sivakami. Your uncle committed a blunder by sending a great warrior like you to learn devotional songs and sculpt boulders!'

'Sculpting is a divine art, aiyya!'

'Enough of that! Mahendra chakravarthy has brought the Pallava empire to its current state by saying such things. Even I am going to petition to the chakravarthy as follows, "Please refrain from creating sculptures out of mountains and rocks. Ask all the sculptors in the Pallava kingdom to build Bharata mandapams in every village, where people should congregate and listen to discourses on the Mahabharata."'

'Why is all this necessary?' asked Paranjyothi.

'This war cannot be won solely by Mahendra chakravarthy and the army. The citizens of the Pallava empire must also be motivated. They must be willing to give up their lives.'

Before Vajrabahu left Paranjyothi, he affectionately hugged the youth and said, 'Thambi, I have a son of your age. If you befriend each other, both of you will scale great heights!'

Paranjyothi, who was overcome by emotion, stammered, 'Aiyya! I lost my father when I was young. Please accept me as your son!'

* * *

After Vajrabahu left Paranjyothi and entered the army camp, each passing moment seemed to be an eon to Paranjyothi. He waited impatiently for orders from the chakravarthy to fetch him.

Within a few minutes, the Pallava army camp turned tumultuous. Suddenly, the mountains echoed with the din of thousands of soldiers cheering and proclaiming victory, and with fireworks. The sound from conches, trumpets and drums reached the sky.

Paranjyothi, who was standing by the entrance of the army camp, hesitantly approached the guards there and enquired the reason for the festivity.

The enthusiastic response was, 'Mahendra Pallava chakravarthy has arrived at the army camp!'

* * *

To be continued . . .

Glossary

Tamil Months

Cittirai	mid-April to mid-May
Vaikasi	mid-May to mid-June
Ani	mid-June to mid-July
Aṭi	mid-July to mid-August
Avaṇi	mid-August to mid-September
Puraṭṭasi	mid-September to mid-October
Aippasi	mid-October to mid-November
Karthikai	mid-November to mid-December
Markazhi	mid-December to mid-January
Thai	mid-January to mid-February
Masi	mid-February to mid-March
Pankuni	mid-March to mid-April

Distance

1 kadu	Approximately 10 miles or 16 kilometres

Units of Time

1 nazhigai	24 minutes
1 muhurtham	48 minutes
1 jaamam	2 hours, 24 minutes
10 jaamams	1 day